It Had to Be YOU

Also by Jill Churchill

GRACE & FAVOR MYSTERIES

Anything Goes

In the Still of the Night

Someone to Watch Over Me

Love for Sale

JANE JEFFRY MYSTERIES

Grime and Punishment

A Farewell to Yarns

A Quiche Before Dying

The Class Menagerie

A Knife to Remember

From Here to Paternity

Silence of the Hams

War and Peas

Fear of Frying

A Groom with a View

Merchant of Menace

Mulch Ado About Nothing

The House of Seven Mabels

Bell, Book, and Scandal

*Jill Churchill can be reached
at her website www.cozybooks.com*

It Had to Be

YOU

A Grace & Favor Mystery

JILL CHURCHILL

WILLIAM MORROW
An Imprint of HarperCollins*Publishers*

Designed by Adrian Leichter

ISBN 0-06-052843-5

CHAPTER ONE

Friday, March 3, 1933

Here's another one," Lily said, putting a letter down on Mr. Prinney's desk at his secondary office at Grace and Favor.

This one was on brown bag paper, carefully folded and addressed to The Honerable Mr. Horatio Bruster.

Mr. Prinney carefully pulled it apart.

Written on the inside of the envelope to save wasting paper, it said,

> *Deer Sir, my wife is writing this for me. I aint got much edication. But Im a darned good farmer. Sad to say that the hale kilt our been crop last fall and we aint had no rain atall this year. We're sorry we havent payed the morgage for a cuple months now but hope you understand. We will try to pay as soon as we kan. We hope its gonna rain this year.*
> *Jimmy Brubaker in Gardan City Kansas*

This was the sixth letter they'd received this spring. Most of them said virtually the same thing.

Lily and Robert's great-uncle Horatio had bought great tracts of land in Nebraska, Colorado, Kansas, and Oklahoma long before the stock market crashed, and sold it to farmers. For the first four years the venture had been profitable. But the good weather had turned bad in 1929, and had progressively become worse. There hadn't been rain for two or three years.

Mr. Prinney, the executor of Horatio Brewster's estate, sighed. "Lily, would you write back. The usual wording." Which was that Mr. Brewster had passed on and that Mr. Prinney was in charge of the estate on behalf of Mr. Brewster's great-niece and great-nephew. On their behalf he was communicating that the mortgage payments didn't have to be paid this year, and that the penalty clause in the contract would not be enforced. He hoped the weather would get better this summer and that the mortgage holder could resume payments next year.

While Lily was typing the letter to Mr. Brubaker, Robert was preparing to go to Washington, D.C., to see President-elect Franklin Roosevelt's inauguration. Even Mr. Prinney reluctantly agreed that Robert deserved the trip. On Election Day the previous November, Robert had worked every hour the polls were open, driving around town in his beloved Duesenberg and gathering up loads of voters, who got the car so dirty it took him nearly a week to get it clean again.

He was this very day standing with a huge crowd at the Hyde Park railroad station watching Roosevelt being lifted into his private train in his wheelchair by his sons. Hundreds of people from surrounding counties cheered as the next president appeared at the window of the train. The mobs of photographers hadn't taken his picture until then. Roosevelt was leaning out of the open window, waving, and grinning with his cigarette holder in his mouth. Robert was waving back madly.

When the train pulled out and Roosevelt's window was closed against the cinders and smoke from the coal, some of the people drifted away. Many more, including Robert, waited patiently with their tickets for the next train to pull into the station, and piled on gleefully to follow. Robert snagged his reserved seat that he'd booked weeks earlier, and realized how thirsty he was. He hadn't had anything to eat or drink since going to bed the night before, for fear he might have to give up his seat to go to the bathroom and lose his place to some of the people jostling him in the aisle.

A small price to pay, he thought.

He'd consulted the alumini address list his college sent out every year to graduates and discovered that several old acquaintances from his school days had moved to Washington, D.C., and hoped he could bunk down with one of them for a couple of days. He'd even managed to find a Washington phone book at the Voorburg library and looked up their phone numbers. It was two years old, but a few friends were certainly still at the same place.

When the train arrived in Washington, he found a bathroom first, washed his hands, and bought a sandwich and a cup of very bad coffee. Then he gathered his change and found a pay phone. The first number he tried didn't answer. Neither did the second. The third old friend answered on the third ring.

"James, this is Robert Brewster. A voice from the past. I'm down here to watch the inauguration. I wondered if I could sleep on your sofa or floor for a couple of days?"

"Robert Brewster?" the voice asked. "I remember you. Have you gone mad? Why would you want to come here for that? Most of us campaigned and voted for Hoover and wouldn't waste the time. In fact, I'm just going out of town to avoid the radical Commie crowds. I can't help you out."

Two more phones weren't answered. One number was answered by a woman who'd never heard of him. The next number was no longer in service. The only other person he reached said much the same as the first had. This old school chum said he was sick at heart at Roosevelt's winning.

Robert was disappointed. He'd have to find some fleabag hotel. Or sleep in a homeless shelter. He cringed at the idea of what a shelter would smell like. He'd rather buy a blanket and sleep in a park somewhere.

There was a knock on the front door of Grace and Favor, and Lily went to see who it was. They weren't expecting company. A smiling young man with curly red hair was standing there. Behind him was an odd vehicle, designed like a smaller version of a Greyhound bus, but without the windows down the sides. It was white with a painted sign on the side saying "Kelly Connor's Notions."

"I hope I'm not disturbing you, but I have some things in my bus that you might not be able to find anywhere close by. May I bring my sample case inside?"

Mrs. Prinney had also heard the knock on the door and now appeared behind Lily. "I'd like to see what you have. Come on in, young man," she said, glancing at the small bus.

Lily had been about to tell him she didn't have time and close the door on him.

He scurried back to his bus and returned with a small suitcase. "Wait till you see all the good things I have in here."

"Let's go to the kitchen," Mrs. Prinney said, leading the way. Mrs. Prinney loved company of any kind or age.

She gave the big wooden table a swipe with a cloth,

although it was almost as clean as an operating table. "Sit yourselves down."

Kelly Connor opened the suitcase and it held a virtual cornucopia of sample-sized products. Ball Band galoshes that would fit dolls in brown, blue, red, gray, and green. Tiny cans of Old Dutch cleanser. Three small tubes of Tangee lipstick.

Mimi, their maid, had heard them talking and came into the kitchen with her platinum blond hair tied up with a blue kerchief with only her bangs showing. "Oh, what I'd give for a tube of Tangee. I absolutely love the smell and taste of it," she said, pulling out a chair to sit with them.

"Keep one then," Kelly said, grinning. "I have lots of the full size in my bus. The only thing I don't carry around is the real galoshes, because they come is so many sizes and colors that I don't have room in the bus." He handed the second lipstick to Lily, who opened it and took a deep, satisfying sniff.

Mrs. Prinney demurred. "My husband doesn't like me to wear lipstick."

"He'll hardly notice. It's a very light color," Kelly said. "It's not goopy. It just stains your lips a very light pink. C'mon, try it, madam," he said with a naughty grin.

She went into the hall, applied a bit sparingly, and looked in the mirror. "You're right, young man. I'll take a real tube," she said as she came back to the kitchen.

"So will I," Lily said.

Mimi chimed in, "Me, too. But what does it cost?"

"Only fifteen cents. It would cost twice as much in a shop—if you had a shop in Voorburg that sold it," Kelly said.

He proceeded to pull out other samples. Little bound pieces of Martex towels in many pretty colors. "Just put these up to your cheeks and feel how soft they are," he urged the three women. Next was a small box of Bisquick.

"What's that?" Mrs. Prinney asked.

"It's to make pancakes, biscuits, topping for fruit desserts. It's already got the baking powder in it. Just the right amount."

"I've never heard of such a thing," Mrs. Prinney said. "Lily, read the recipes on the side of the box. They're too tiny and I don't have my glasses."

Lily did so. "You just add milk for things like pancakes or sugar for dessert. You can make almost anything. How big is a real box of this and what does it cost?"

"Only twenty cents for a box about this big," Kelly said, making a gesture. "I could go to my bus and show you a real box if you want to see one."

"Later," Mrs. Prinney said. "What else is in there?"

He pulled out a packet of Fleischmann's yeast. "It's good for your health, especially in the winter when there isn't much sunshine."

Next were three tiny bottles of Listerine, packets of Sanka coffee, small tubes of Colgate toothpaste. A little box of Fels-Naptha soap. A packet of Tums. "Very good for indigestion," he said.

"Nobody gets indigestion from my cooking," Emmaline Prinney said rather sharply.

"I'm sure they don't," Kelly Connor said, "but what if you have to eat someone else's cooking?"

He went on removing other things from his suitcase. Samples of Ovaltine, Aqua Velva shaving cream, Wrigley Doublemint chewing gum. Even miniature bars of Baby Ruth candy bars.

At that point Mr. Prinney was drawn in by the giggles coming from the kitchen. "What's this all about?" he asked.

"This young man is showing us samples of things we can't buy unless we go to a big city. This is my husband," Mrs. Prinney said to Kelly. "Mr. Prinney, Esquire."

"And they're all a lot cheaper to buy from me, sir," said Kelly, who had stood up politely when the attorney walked into the kitchen. I've got something in my bus you should know about. Would you mind waiting while I get it?"

A moment later he was back with a big machine. "Sir, this is a mimeograph machine. For your business it would be a really useful thing." He cleared an area of the big kitchen table and set the machine down. He handed Mr. Prinney a double set of papers and said, "Write something down, sir, on the top page. Press a bit hard."

Prinney, in spite of his reservations, wrote a few lines of the Gettysburg Address and handed it back.

Kelly separated the sheets, put the back one down on a roller, and cranked a handle, and several copies of what Mr. Prinney had written came out the other end of the machine, smelling very odd. "The stink goes away pretty soon," Kelly said.

Mr. Prinney waved one of the sheets around to get rid of the odor, and asked, "How many of these could you make with this thing?"

"At least twenty before it starts to get hazy. Want me to show you?"

"No need to," Mr. Prinney said stiffly. "I'll take your word." He'd been disapproving of this nonsense when the machine was hauled in, but now there was a light in his eye.

It didn't take Mr. Prinney very long to come back to his senses. He had a secretary who had strong enough fingers to type three copies at once by using carbon papers. He couldn't think of any occasion when he'd need twenty copies of anything.

CHAPTER TWO

Saturday, March 4

Robert woke up at dawn shivering. He'd spent the night on the grounds of the East Plaza of the Capitol with thousands of other people far better equipped than he was for a nippy night. He'd already located a public bathroom where he could shave in the morning. There was no mirror and only cold water. He left his blanket and small pillow in place, hoping no one would steal it or take over his spot. The day was overcast and cold and there was a brisk wind cutting through his clothes. He should have worn a coat.

Most of the others attending had planned better. They were in pickup trucks with beds and warm bedding in the back. Many had tents along with kerosene lanterns and heaters. There were hundreds of children running around unsupervised, stepping on the hands and feet of the unfortunate, like Robert, who were trying to sleep on the ground. He estimated he might have had two full hours of sleep altogether. He staggered to the bathroom, where he shaved, washed his face, and slicked back his hair, shivering.

Eventually the ceremony took place on a balcony of the Capitol. The crowd stood shoulder to shoulder and had grown at least three times in size since the night before. They all fell silent while Franklin Roosevelt took the oath of office.

When the ceremony was finished, fifty thousand people cheered before dispersing to follow the parade to the White House. Robert learned later that, counting the many groups marching in the parade and the people watching the parade along the route, the inauguration involved almost a half million participants. The whole city was draped in flags, the endless string of marching bands creating quite a din as they played different music at the same time.

Finally Roosevelt appeared on the balcony at the White House and gave a rousing speech. By that time Robert was so exhausted, he was hard-pressed to remember what was said, though as the words washed over him, he thought it was a grand speech. The only part he remembered clearly was the best: "The only thing we have to fear is fear itself."

Surely Jack Summer, the editor of the *Voorburg-on-Hudson Times,* would reprint the speech and Robert could more fully enjoy it in the warmth and comfort of Grace and Favor. He picked up his valise and staggered toward the train station, wondering why he'd thought this such a good idea. Maybe when he was an old man, he'd remember it fondly and bore his grandchildren to death repeating the story year after year.

He hoped to sleep all the way back to Voorburg but discovered that he'd lost his reserved-seat ticket somehow and had to stand the whole time.

He took the only town taxi back up the hill, and though the driver always scared him to death, the way he drove so fast and recklessly up the narrow winding road to Grace and Favor, Robert fell fast asleep before they even started the ascent.

"Robert, you look awful," Lily said as the taxi driver dragged Robert through the front door. Lily had been on her way down the stairs. She approached him cautiously. "You're not drunk, are you?"

"I'm not," he said, slurring his words. "I'm just tired. Could you help me upstairs?"

"Are you ill?" Now Lily was seriously worried. She'd never seen him so hangdog. He had apparently tried to shave and nicked himself all over his chin. His hair was in complete disarray. He looked and smelled like a bum.

She paid the taxi driver, then took Robert by the elbow

and led him upstairs to his room. "I'm running you a bath," she said.

"I'll drown," he whimpered.

"You won't. You need a good long sleep, but frankly, you stink of trains and stale popcorn and something else I can't identify."

"Woman. Awful perfume. Next to me. Train," he said pathetically as he watched the water filling the tub.

Ten minutes later, at nine o'clock in the evening, she put him to bed. He hadn't even toweled off the water. When he came back out of the bathroom, his pajamas were damp. *He'll dry out in bed,* Lily thought.

Then she went back down the stairs to alert everyone to leave Robert alone until the next day. Mimi was disappointed. "I thought he'd be gone longer. I need to do a good turnout of his room."

"Not until I say so," Lily said firmly.

She got up several times during the night to check that he was still alive. Given that he was snoring loudly each time, she assumed he was all right.

He was still snoring at ten o'clock Sunday morning. She knocked on the door and said, "Time to get up, Robert."

"Huhhh?" was his only reply.

She opened the door and saw that he was still in the same position she'd put him in the night before. "You'll

stiffen up like a corpse if you don't move around a little."
She grabbed one of his arms to get him vertical.

He looked around the room and at Lily as if he didn't quite know who she was or where he was. Then he groaned as he feebly pushed aside the sheets and bedspread and swung his legs to the ground. He had to keep one hand on the mattress to get upright. "I feel two hundred years old."

"You only look ninety," Lily said with a smile. "What happened to you?"

"I haven't slept since I left here," he mumbled, testing his footing. "I tried, but a hundred and fifty people stepped on me. Maybe more. I lost my reserved-seat train ticket and had to stand all the way home until I fell into the taxi."

"But did you enjoy anything?"

"I wouldn't have missed it, even if I'd known what a misery I'd be in afterward," he said with a halfhearted smile that changed to pain when his facial muscles moved. He felt his chin. "What have I done to myself?"

"You shaved badly. Yesterday I purchased an ointment for burns and cuts. I bet that will help your chin. Now clean up, get dressed, and come and eat something. You need nourishment."

"You might have to hold my spoon," he said. "I used to be able to stay up all night dancing and drinking at parties and still play polo the next day. What has happened to me since then?"

She had no good answer, so she left the room so that he could get dressed.

Half an hour later Robert appeared in the kitchen, looking much more like himself. His hair was washed and combed. He'd shaved, all but his sore chin. Lily applied the pungent ointment she and Mrs. Prinney had bought for the household from Kelly Connor. Robert didn't like the smell but admitted it made his chin feel a lot better.

"We've been offered another job," Lily said, sitting down across from him while Mrs. Prinney was making him pancakes with the Bisquick she'd purchased.

"It doesn't start today, does it?" Robert asked.

"Not for you. I'm working it out today with Miss Twibell."

"Who's she?"

"She has the mansion just north of us. You've seen her. She brought two of her ladies to the Fate once. The heavy one who walked with two sticks, remember? And the smaller one."

"I have a vague recollection. The lady with the sticks was funny. I chatted with her a bit and found her a chair. She sat knitting and making jokes with the children. What do you mean about 'two of her ladies'?"

"She's turned her big house into a nursing home. She called this morning saying she'd heard from Mrs. Tarkington that we'd taken over teaching for the missing teacher

for a couple weeks and wondered if we'd help her out for a
while at the nursing home."

"For pay?" Robert asked.

"Yes. That's what I need to discuss with her. She's having trouble with her bunions, she said, and one of the
young women who work for her is out sick with the flu."

"This won't involve anything nasty, will it? We don't
empty bedpans or wash out nasty wounds, do we?"

"I'll make sure we don't," Lily said with a shudder. "I
need to get over there soon."

"Want me to drive you?"

"I wouldn't ride with you in the condition you're in. I'll
walk. It's not far."

Robert looked relieved. Normally any excuse to swan
around in the big butter-yellow Duesie appealed to him—
except today.

Lily was shivering as she approached the house. She'd
only worn an ordinary coat and wished she'd put on her
tatty old sable one. In spite of the cold, she was impressed
at how well fitted out this house was. It wasn't quite as big
as Grace and Favor but was still a substantial three-story
brick house. The drive was a perfection of small stones,
carefully raked. Along the side of the drive, the little
points of tulips were just poking up through the ground.
There were the ghosts of gardens starting to grow around
the front. To the side, a small grove of what appeared to
be some kind of fruit trees had a faint green flush of

green. Well-kept grass was just greening up as well. And freshly painted dark blue shutters on all the windows made the white of the painted bricks sparkle, even on a cold, dreary day.

Miss Twibell must have had the money to keep up the house and grounds better than they could manage at Grace and Favor. The front door was opened by a pretty young Negro woman, wearing a freshly pressed housedress with a flowered pattern. A little boy was at her side.

"You must be Miss Brewster. I'm Doreen, the laundress. I'm filling in on 'door duty' for Mattie, who's out sick. Miss Twibell is confined to the second floor what with her bunions acting up. She said you could go straight up."

"Thank you, Doreen. What a cute little boy you have. What's his name?"

"Buddy. Really Sam. But he's my buddy, aren't you, honey-child?" The little boy smiled and hid his face in her apron.

Lily went up the center flight of stairs and found Miss Twibell waiting in a chair in the middle of the central hallway. "Are you doing any better yet?" Lily asked.

"Not much," Miss Twibell said, getting to her feet with a grimace. "They flare up about this time every year. It must be the change in weather. Let me introduce you to our people. Then we'll talk about what I need and what I'll pay."

"I already met Doreen and Buddy downstairs," Lily

said, offering her arm as support, which Miss Twibell took gratefully.

Lily had only seen her briefly at the Fate, but not in her crisp white starched uniform with the upside-down watch on her bodice and the stethoscope around her neck. Miss Twibell might have been anywhere between thirty-five and forty-five. She was taller than Lily, a little heavier, and had dark blond hair in a neat bun at the back of her neck with a net over it.

They entered an open door to a big living room with a warm pink carpet and two sofas and three comfy-looking chairs with a good antique table by each. In front of the sofa was big low table with newspapers and magazines in neat piles, as well as a vase of pink hothouse tulips, half them still in bud, the rest in bloom. Lily assumed Miss Twibell probably had a substantial private income to afford such flowers.

At the far end of the huge room, there were sparkling white cabinets with locks on the glass doors, containing an array of bandages, splints, bottles, and boxes, above a white counter. This area had a painted white floor. A wooden wheelchair stood in a corner. A door at the right side was probably to a storeroom. Everything looked and smelled spotlessly clean. Miss Twibell was a real professional. Being temporarily crippled and without part of her staff, she must have been at her wit's end to keep it so pristine yet cozy.

"I'll introduce you to my patients now. We'll get the worst over with first," Miss Twibell said in a whisper. They entered a room with a chart on the door. A young woman was standing at the opposite side of a hospital bed with a tented white sheet propped up, apparently bathing an old man's knee.

"Miss Brewster, this is Betty."

Betty glanced up and smiled briefly, saying, "Glad to meet you, Miss Brewster," before reaching to a rolling table next to her and picking up a cotton swab with shiny tongs and dabbing it on the man's knee.

"And this is Mr. Sean Connor. Meet Miss Brewster, Mr. Connor. We're hoping she and her brother can do us the favor of filling in for me and Mattie for a while."

The man looked around the tented sheet and glared at Lily. "I don't like strangers in my room." He was smallish and wrinkled but had a strong, abrasive voice.

"Tut-tut. Don't be rude," Miss Twibell said. "She won't be a stranger for long." Then she went around the bed and looked at the knee and said to Betty, "Good job, dear."

They left his room. "I see what you mean," Lily said. "He's not very pleasant. Is he seriously ill?"

"I'm afraid he is. He broke his knee and it's become badly inflamed. We had to lance it and now we clean it four times a day at least."

"Connor?" Lily asked. "I met a Kelly Connor the day before yesterday. Any relation to your patient?"

"Grandson," Miss Twibell replied. "He drops in when he can to visit his grandpa. He brings him samples of all sorts of things. He puts them on the table next to his bed, but Mr. Connor seldom uses them, except for the cigars. Come along now and meet my two ladies. They're another kettle of fish."

CHAPTER THREE

The next two patients were a treat. Miss Jones and Miss Smith were delighted to see her. They carried on about how pretty Lily was before Miss Twibell could even tell them who Lily was.

"Ladies, this is Miss Lily Brewster. She lives at Grace and Favor—"

"That handsome, charming Robert Brewster must be your brother then," Miss Smith said. Lily had recognized her by her weight and the sticks standing beside her bed. She was sitting in a chair, surrounded by pillows, with her feet up on an ottoman. A pair of well-polished wooden walking sticks were close to her chair.

"Not today he isn't," Lily said. "I mean, he's my brother today. But he isn't handsome or charming right now. That's why he's not with me."

"Chicken pox, I'll bet," put in the much thinner lady sitting in the chair next to the other bed. Both were fully dressed, hosed, and shod. Miss Smith was even wearing a little bit of lipstick.

"Not quite," Lily said with a laugh and went on to explain what had happened to Robert in the two days before.

"He actually saw President Roosevelt in person!" Miss Jones said, with a slight cough finishing the statement.

"You've seen him, too, and so have I," Miss Smith said to her friend. "Are you becoming forgetful?"

"Of course not, Eulalia, but I haven't seen him as the President of the United States. By the way, Miss Brewster, I'm Francine Jones. I was at the Fate with Eulalia. But you won't have noticed me. Nobody does when she's around," she said with another little laugh and a lighter cough following it.

"You two have ruined my introduction," Miss Twibell said with mock anger. "I knew you would."

"You may call us by our first names when we're all here in this room, dear," Miss Smith said. "It wouldn't do in public, of course. As we are much older than you." Lily guessed that "public" included the large living room.

"You both have lovely first names. How did you come by them?" Lily asked. She couldn't sit down because there was only one other chair and Miss Twibell had subsided onto it to get off her feet.

"Eulalia was my grandmother on my father's side," Miss Smith said, beginning what sounded as if it might

22

turn into a very long story. "She met my grandfather when he was in New Orleans on business, and agreed practically on the same day to marry him and come north. She regretted it the rest of her life, I think. She wouldn't set a foot outside when it was cold. She even refused to ever buy a heavy coat or winter boots. She once went to a play in town in a blizzard wearing only her velvet cloak and had to take to her bed for three days after."

Miss Jones was making a "blab-blab-blab" gesture with her right hand and holding on to the stitch she was knitting with her left.

That's when Lily realized that both of them had their hands occupied with knitting. She noted at the same time that there were shelves on the side wall with a great many hanks and balls of yarn as well as several projects that were completed and folded neatly. This, too, was a large bedroom, easily big enough for two ladies to share.

Before Miss Smith could go on about her grandmother, Lily turned to Miss Jones. "And your name? Where did you get it?"

Miss Jones took a deep, slightly raspy breath, and said, "My mother and father traveled to France for their honeymoon and loved the girls' names." She managed it without coughing after she spoke.

Miss Twibell rose to her feet gingerly and said, "Miss Brewster and I need to have a private talk."

Goodbyes were said, in great detail by Miss Smith,

before the other two women could get away. The young woman named Betty was sitting in the main room, reading a magazine. "Could you hold down the fort while I have a talk with Miss Brewster?" Miss Twibell asked her.

"I'd be glad to. I've read this magazine before. I just looked in on Mr. Connor again. He's sleeping peacefully, but still running two degrees of fever."

Miss Twibell took Lily out into the hall and said, "We'll go to my private sitting room. There are speaking tubes with bells everywhere in the place that can ring me there if I'm needed."

Lily remembered when Robert's friend, known to them as "Mad Henry," had tried to set up a system like this at Grace and Favor. His idea had been a disaster, but had nonetheless helped to solve a mystery. Lily assumed that Miss Twibell's speaking tubes worked more efficiently than Mad Henry's.

Miss Twibell's sitting room was lovely in an old-fashioned way. Two large sofas flanked a big fireplace, and a group of chairs and a table were arranged by a large window through which Lily could see the grounds outside the back of the home. This is where Miss Twibell seated them.

"I see that Mr. Farleigh, my other patient, is already doing his first mowing," she said, glancing outside. Lily looked. A thin man wearing corduroy trousers, a white shirt, a blue vest, and a brown tweed jacket was pushing a

mower around below the window. She could just barely
hear the snick of the blades as he moved.

"Well, what do you think?" Miss Twibell asked. She
named a figure she'd pay each of them per day that was
reasonable but by no means extravagant.

"What will you expect us to do?" Lily asked.

"I'd like one or both of you to take the laundry down
and bring it back. I have an assortment of wicker baskets.
You could take some light loads down and back this afternoon if you're free to stay the rest of the day."

"Of course I am," Lily agreed.

Miss Twibell went on, "I think your brother, when he's
feeling better, could take bigger baskets, and entertain
Miss Smith and Miss Jones." She immediately followed
this with the beginning of an apology. "I know they're
charming, but if I hear one more time how Eulalia got her
name—and you heard only a small portion of the story of
her mother—I'll go raving mad if these bunions don't stop
hurting."

"It's right down Robert's alley. He's good with old
ladies. Even ones he doesn't like. He has a gift for acting as
if he's listening intently while his mind is somewhere else
entirely."

"Good. Now that Betty is so occupied with Mr. Connor's knee treatments, you might take on some of the dusting and mopping, if you don't mind. It's not hard. I also

have a long dry mop for the cobwebs, which are always a problem in old houses. I'm convinced the webs hold on to germs."

"I never thought about that. They probably do." Lily knew that their maid, Mimi, was always after cobwebs. She wondered if it was because of germs or because Mimi hated spiders.

"Fair warning, though," Miss Twibell went on, "I use a very strong soap on the floors. I'll supply you with gloves to protect your hands from shriveling up. And it requires two complete mop-ups to keep my painted area from getting slippery."

"I'll keep that in mind," Lily said. "How often do the floors get cleaned?"

"I like them to be done twice a day. But beggars can't be choosers. Once is really sufficient unless something gets spilled. Usually Betty does one round first thing in the morning and Mattie does it late in the afternoon. Mattie's the one who is home sick. You can take over in the afternoon for her."

Lily was thinking that she'd go through with it for the money. But mopping and dusting were a bit foreign to her. Cleaning it was Mimi's obsession. Miss Twibell would be better off with Mimi. But then Grace and Favor would suffer. And what if Mimi found the scope of cleaning at the nursing home gave her more pleasure and left Grace and Favor? How could they ever replace her?

Lily put this thought aside and said, "If you'll tell me where the smaller baskets are and where the dirty linens are, I'll start right now."

Miss Twibell sighed happily and gave her directions. Then she said, "If you can't find them, ask Betty. I really need to stay off my feet for a little longer."

Lily thought of "small" baskets as handbaskets. Miss Twibell's view of "small" baskets was more generous. They were the size of suitcases without tops. The large baskets in the storeroom were almost the size of traveling trunks. Lily was exhausted by the end of the day. From now on, Robert could haul them up and down to the basement. The mopping was easier, though the smell of the soap was very strong. Still, as she contemplated walking home, she was proud of having done two-thirds of a day's fairly hard work. The exercise would be good for her, she told herself.

As she started out the front door, she realized that the house itself had been so warm that it seemed terribly cold outside. She wished even more that she'd worn her old sable coat. She went back inside and asked Miss Twibell's permission to call Robert to pick her up. He was there in moments, having recovered from his trip, and jabbering a mile a minute the whole way home. He'd been glued to the radio all afternoon. "Lily, Roosevelt sure moves fast. Today he closed all the banks in the country. His first day in office and he's already making changes."

"Robert, pull over for a minute and let me get one of those car blankets out of the backseat." When she was bundled up and they were on their way again, she asked, "Is that a good idea? Closing banks?"

"Of course it is. They've been going down like ninepins. Stronger banking regulations need to be drawn up."

"Can't anyone get their money out? What if you needed to pay bills and you couldn't?" Lily asked.

"The banks are allowed to make change, make loans for human and animal food, let safe-deposit boxes be opened, and accept payments due them. They can't give out money. Everybody's supposed to turn in any gold coins they have. They can get money that way."

"How many people do you know who have a pocket or handbag full of gold coins?" Lily asked.

"Not many ordinary people. But the rich have them."

"Right," Lily replied cynically. "Robert, drive a little bit faster. I'm freezing." She could hardly believe she'd said that. She was usually begging him to drive slower.

Lily went to take a nice hot bath to get the smell of soap off her skin and out of her hair, then cornered Robert. "We need to talk about this job over breakfast."

"Okay," he said, preoccupied with fiddling with the radio in the library. He looked up suddenly. "They do have a radio there I can listen to, don't they? That's really all I need."

"There was one in the living room area," Lily said. "But nobody was listening. Maybe it doesn't work."

"If it doesn't and I can't fix it, I'll have to buy a small one to leave there."

"Mrs. Prinney has one, I think. Maybe she'd lend it to you," Lily said. "If not, you could hunt around in the basement. You've found lots of things down there."

Mimi came into the library to say that she was ready to put dinner on the table.

CHAPTER FOUR

Monday, March 6

As Lily and Robert were eating breakfast before going to the nursing home, Robert asked, "How many people does this Miss Twibell have as patients?"

"Only four. She has an extra room for an emergency patient and two rooms for the young nurses who help her. Two old ladies share one big room, and will talk the socks off you. One cranky old man, and one man I haven't seen except from above. He was mowing the backyard."

"If he can mow a yard, why is he a patient?"

Lily shrugged.

"How many are on the staff?"

"The two young nurses who help the patients and change the bedding and bandages. One of them is sick, which is why Miss Twibell needs us. Apparently the two of us equal one of her," Lily said with a wry smile. "There's also a woman who lives in the basement with her child and does the laundry. And Dr. Polhemus is on call. And does routine visits."

Robert frowned. "I'm surprised she uses him. He's such an awful gossip. I'll bet the whole town knows every detail of the four patients' symptoms."

"Who else could she get locally?" Lily asked. "I don't imagine her budget allows for a full-time doctor to live there. Oh, there's also a cook and an assistant for her. I wasn't introduced, so I don't know their names. Cook sent the assistant up with the trays."

"Is she a good cook?" Robert asked.

"Yes, I think so. She sent up the best chicken soup I've ever had. It also had big fat egg noodles added for everyone but Mr. Connor. He got the plain soup. There were tuna sandwiches with lots of celery and good bread as well."

"We only take that one meal, right?"

"You just had your breakfast, Robert. And I ate dinner here last night. Didn't you notice? There must be part-time local women who come in and clean everything but the hospital part of the nursing home.

"As for the patients, Miss Smith has bad hips and has to walk with sticks," Lily added. "She knows who you are and is smitten."

"I think you told me about her before."

"I probably did. I'm guessing the woman who shares

her room has asthma. Mr. Connor has a broken knee that's apparently badly infected."

"Connor? Any relation to the young man Mrs. Prinney told me about who sold you all that stuff while I was gone? Oh, you must have bought those three packs of cigarettes that were on my night table from him. Thanks."

"You're welcome. The young man is Kelly Connor, Mr. Connor's grandson."

"What's Miss Twibell like? Aside from having bunions?"

"I'll let you form your own opinion. We're supposed to be there at nine."

When they arrived, Doreen had to let them in again. Lily introduced Robert to Doreen and Buddy, who was again hiding against his mother's apron, peeking at them.

"Go on up," Doreen said. "I'm told there's a problem with one of the patients, which is why Betty didn't open the door," she explained to Robert.

"I step in just as there's a 'problem,'" Robert groaned quietly.

"It's not our responsibility, Robert. Don't fret," Lily said as they went up the stairway.

When they arrived in the living room, Mr. Connor's door was open. Miss Twibell was wearing her carpet slippers instead of real shoes, and standing over Mr. Connor. Betty was beside her. They were talking in low voices.

"Robert," Lily said quietly, "I'll show you where the laundry baskets are and where to take them. When we get back, I'll tackle cleaning the floors and counter and you can entertain Miss Smith and Miss Jones. That will keep both of us out from underfoot."

Apparently, this was the day that the bulk of the linens were washed. Lily took the small basket and Robert wrestled the huge one down the stairs. "They *really* need an elevator," he said. "Or one of those dumbwaiters. I'll bet the Harbinger boys would know how to install it."

"I wouldn't suggest that right away if I were you," Lily said.

They had to make three trips to get everything down to the basement.

Robert stayed in the basement to play the little radio he'd found in a cabinet under the stairs at Grace and Favor and brought along. Buddy listened, too, while Doreen started the first load of washing.

Lily went upstairs and started mopping the pharmacy part of the largest room. Betty was sound asleep on the sofa. Miss Twibell came into the big sitting room. "I didn't even notice you were here," she said wearily. "Is your brother along today?"

"Yes. He'll be back from the basement in a few minutes. How is Mr. Connor doing?" They were both whispering so they wouldn't wake Betty.

"Badly. He always pretends he's in a coma when his wife visits. But I'm afraid it's almost true today. He's mean as a cob. I hope he at least goes gently. Betty has been mon-

JILL CHURCHILL

itoring his blood pressure and pulse every three hours overnight. That's why she's taking a nap."

Watching Lily wash the floor, she pulled up a chair and took off her carpet slippers and gently massaged her feet.

"I remember their wedding," she said softly. "Mr. and Mrs. Connor's. I was just a girl then and my parents took me along. Mrs. Connor was the happiest bride I'd ever seen. She couldn't stop smiling the whole time. When they turned to come down the aisle, Mr. Connor looked as if somebody had hit him with half a brick. He looked terrified at what he'd just done. She was at least a head taller than he was and must have outweighed him by twenty pounds."

Lily smiled and started the first round of rinsing the floor.

Putting one carpet slipper back on, Miss Twibell went on, "I guess she kept track of my family. At least well enough to know I run a nursing home. She put him in here about three months ago and visits him every week. Things have changed with them. All she does is berate him while she's here."

"What about?" Lily ventured to ask, even though it was none of her business.

"Their son Stefan and Stefan's sons. Apparently there was a big family blowup many years ago and Stefan moved to the other side of Beacon, refusing to be in touch with them and also refusing to let them see their grandsons."

34

"I thought you said Kelly Connor visited his grandfather when he was in Voorburg and gave him samples?"

"Yes. But never when his grandmother is around. And he asked me to keep his visits secret from her. Which I've done. He visited this morning, in fact. He knows his grandmother doesn't come until around eleven. And the visiting nurse turned up early, too."

She sighed and donned her other carpet slipper and stood up. "Enough gossiping. I don't know what's come over me."

As she spoke, Robert came into the main room and said, "I just heard on the radio that Mayor Cermak died today."

Both Lily and Miss Twibell shushed him, pointing at Betty.

"Oh, the poor man. Having to linger like that for three weeks," Miss Twibell said quietly. "It's a shame, but good that the assassin didn't shoot our new President as he meant to."

"It was a close thing," Robert said. "Roosevelt had just given a speech and was still standing in his car. Cermak was standing on the running board."

"Miss Twibell," Lily said, "I suppose you've guessed that this is my brother, Robert. He didn't give me the chance to be polite."

"I guessed," Miss Twibell said, smiling. "Now I have to get real shoes on. This is the day Mr. Connor's wife visits."

"What's up?" Robert asked when Miss Twibell had gone.

"She thinks he's going into a coma. It must be almost the end for him."

"I don't want to be around for that," Robert admitted. "It would be better to visit the two old ladies. Do you need any help?"

"No, thanks. I'm almost done. I'll tell you when the bell rings to pick up the finished laundry."

"I'll await that as eagerly as you think. Getting it down there was awful. Getting it back up will be worse. You're sure I can't mention an elevator?"

"Not today," Lily replied firmly.

Mrs. Connor arrived an hour later. She walked into her husband's room, leaving the door slightly ajar. The first thing she said was, "Don't think you're fooling me, Sean. I know you're awake. I have some farm problems we need to discuss." There was a silence, then she must have gotten up from the chair next to his bed, realizing she was being heard. She slammed the door and went back to talking. But the words were muffled.

Miss Twibell had been in her suite putting her nurse shoes on and hobbled in just in time to hear this.

Betty was still on the sofa but was now sitting up, rubbing her eyes, still half asleep from being up most of the night checking on Mr. Connor. Miss Twibell sat on a chair next to the sofa, putting her feet up on the center table. They didn't speak.

Lily got busy cleaning the counter now that she'd finished the floor, thinking vaguely that she probably should
do these chores in the opposite way. Counter first, in case
she dropped pieces of lint on the floor. As she finished up
and was heading for the closet to put the mop away, Mrs.
Connor opened the door of her husband's room and
shouted, "He's not breathing!"

Betty and Miss Twibell leaped up and hurried into the
room, Miss Twibell closing it behind them. Even with the
door shut, Lily could hear Mrs. Connor wailing and sobbing. "I really thought he'd get better and come home and
go back to work."

Miss Twibell and Betty brought Mrs. Connor out of
the room and helped her to the sofa. She was still sobbing
and hiccuping. Miss Twibell pushed a bell by the door, and
the cook's assistant showed up in a moment. "We need
three cups of strong tea and sugar, please. As quickly as
you can," Miss Twibell told her.

The girl was back in moments. Mrs. Connor's sobbing
had stopped and she was mopping her eyes and nose with
an oversized handkerchief with a lace border.

"What do I do now?" she asked. "How can I take care
of the farm all by myself any longer? The workers don't
like me. One of them walked out this morning. That's
what I wanted to talk to Sean about."

"Don't worry about that now," Miss Twibell said. She'd

been through this any number of times, comforting bereaved relatives when patients reached the end of their lives. "First, you need to make the funeral arrangements."

"I'll bury him on our land, where all my family are buried," Mrs. Connor said. "That's only right."

"You need to consult his attorney first to see if he had a will leaving instructions as to his wishes," Miss Twibell told her. "Would you like me to call and make you an appointment? I also need to call Dr. Polhemus to sign the death certificate."

"Oh, I hadn't thought of that. Yes, please." Mrs. Connor told her the name of the family attorney.

Lily went to Miss Smith's and Miss Jones's room. She really wasn't entitled to eavesdrop on Mrs. Connor anymore, and didn't want to appear to be doing so.

Miss Smith was laughing uproariously at something Robert had said. Miss Jones was smiling as she was sewing two narrow strips of knitted work together with a curved blunt needle.

"What's so funny?" Lily asked. Miss Smith was laughing so hard she couldn't explain. Robert rose from the one chair and gestured for Lily to sit in the chair, and then said to Miss Jones, "Would it be improper if I sat on the foot of your bed?"

"Better than the floor," Miss Jones wheezed. "You'd get bits of yarn all over your trousers."

They chatted for a half hour but couldn't help hearing a trolley roll into Mr. Connor's room and leave a few minutes later. Lily hadn't intended to tell the pair of old ladies that Mr. Connor was dying. But they guessed when they heard the noises. "He's gone, then?" Miss Jones asked.

"I think so," Lily said.

"Good riddance," Miss Smith said. "He was a nasty man. I have friends in Beacon and they told me years ago about him cheating his oldest son."

"How?" Robert asked.

"Connor and his son Stefan owned a rental property," Miss Smith explained, "or so my friend said. Connor wanted to sell it. The son didn't. So Connor forged his son's name on the deed and sold it anyway. And he kept all the money. His son was furious. Connor's wife took her husband's side and between them they drove the son and grandsons away. From the way we hear her talking to him these days, she must have changed her mind about his morals since then."

Robert heard a bell ring and they went to see if it was Doreen alerting him that the first load of laundry was done. It was and he went away reluctantly, muttering about elevators.

As Lily stood around at loose ends, Betty came out of Mr. Connor's former room, carrying a pillow and sheets.

She took Miss Twibell aside and showed her something. Miss Twibell nodded and headed for the telephone in the main room.

"Give me Chief of Police Howard Walker's number, please," she said to the operator. It took a few minutes for the operator to find him. He wasn't at the boardinghouse where his main office was. She finally located him at the jail.

Miss Twibell said, "Chief Walker, this is Miss Twibell. Could you do me a favor? Would you call over to the funeral home in Beacon and tell them not to do anything to the body that's on the way. We'll need an autopsy done before they embalm him. I could have told them this, but they might consider me a silly woman making something out of nothing. I'd like a chief of police—either you or their own chief in Beacon—to back me up on this. Then come up here and see what my nurse found. Meanwhile, I'll call Dr. Polhemus to tell him not to file the death certificate yet."

"What's happened?" Chief Walker asked.

"I'd rather tell you in person. You know how those girls at the telephone exchange listen in. And I have something you need to see."

Howard had been chatting with Jack Summer when the call came through.

"I'm putting the next newspaper issue together," Jack had said. "Have you had anything I can report?"

"Nothing but two drunk drivers, and one accident due to ice on a driveway back last January. And a boy putting a quarter on the railroad tracks to see if it would derail the train."

"Really boring winter for you, huh? No serious crimes to investigate since that woman bumped off the preacher in November."

"I like it when Voorburg is boring. It makes me feel like I'm a good cop, and the citizens are mostly good people. I'm sticking with the job, even though I had some good offers from bigger cities, thanks to your reporting my arrest in the murder case of a well-known person and passing it on to national newspapers."

"I had a few job offers from that case, too," Jack said. "I also turned them down. I like it here in Voorburg, too."

Howard said, "That might have a little to do with Mrs. Towerton, I suspect."

"Not that that's anybody's business, but I have been courting her from time to time. She keeps trying to pretend it isn't really courting though."

That's when the phone rang.

"What was that about?" Jack asked.

"Miss Twibell at the nursing home wants to tell me something she doesn't want the phone operators to hear."

"May I come along with you? I've already been in touch with her about doing a piece for the paper about the history of the nursing home as part of my series about the old homes on the hill above the village."

"You may come with me, Jack. But if it's serious police business, which it sounds as if it is, you can't report on it until I give you permission."

"Fair enough."

CHAPTER FIVE

Chief Howard Walker came up to the second floor of the nursing home ten minutes after he received Miss Twibell's call, with Jack trailing along, notebook and pencil at the ready. She and Betty took him into the room where Connor had died. Betty showed him the pillow. There was saliva, mucus, and a little blood on it, and a bit of the same on the bottom sheet. Jack was eavesdropping outside the door.

Howard took a look and said, "Someone smothered him with the pillow, then put it back under his head with the nasty side down. Is that what you think?"

"I've seen this happen twice," Miss Twibell said, "when I was a head nurse in New York City. I never thought it could happen here. Chief Walker, I keep my patients safe and as well as I can, and so does my staff."

"I've heard that your reputation is excellent," he assured her. "An autopsy will probably confirm that he was murdered. But the point is, who did it? And when? Gather together your whole staff and the patients if you can and let's try to get the times straight."

He glared when Lily and Robert Brewster escorted the two old ladies to the main room. "What are you two doing here?" he asked the Brewster siblings sharply.

"Helping out Miss Twibell," Lily snapped back.

"Robert, would you round up all the chairs you can find?" Miss Twibell asked. This was not a good time to veer off the subject, even though she was curious about Chief Walker's reaction to seeing the Brewsters. "There are an extra three in my suite you can bring."

She noticed Jack Summer and asked, "What are you doing here? Our appointment for the interview was planned for later in the week."

Jack took her aside and said quietly, "I know that. But Walker let me come with him with my promise of not reporting anything until he gives me permission."

When they were all assembled and seated in a big circle, Howard Walker asked, "Miss Twibell, who was in the victim's room since yesterday?"

"Me, of course. Betty took the night shift checking on him. Quite early this morning the visiting nurse came."

"Who is this visiting nurse, and what time was she here?" Howard asked.

"Miss Lucy Mae Quincy," Miss Twibell said. "She was here from about seven-thirty to seven forty-five. She works for the State of New York in some kind of health department that randomly checks nursing homes. She wasn't on an inspection this time, just calling on me while she was in Voorburg to visit a friend who lives here."

"Is this Miss Quincy a bona fide nurse? Did she go into Mr. Connor's room?" Howard asked.

"She is, and she did. Because I asked her to," Miss Twibell said. "Her opinion agreed with mine that he had only a day or less left. You see, he broke his kneecap falling off a ladder and a severe infection deep in the shattered joint is what would have taken him. The patella, that's the real name for the kneecap, was shattered and pinned together surgically before he came here. Apparently that was when the infection started. We've been cleaning out the wound, alternating peroxide to bubble out the foul matter, and alcohol and sulfa grains to kill the germs, at regular intervals almost the whole time he's been here. There was nothing else we could do."

Jack was standing around the corner of the door to the big room, taking notes madly, hoping no one noticed what he was doing.

Robert cast a pale-faced glance at Lily and she whispered back, "Buck up. It'll soon be over."

Howard said, "Miss Twibell, you don't have to defend yourself. I'm just trying to find out who went into his room."

"Thank you, Chief Walker," she said with relief.

"Just for the record, what does this Miss Quincy usually do when she's here?" Howard asked.

"She swabs various surfaces and puts the swabs in vials that are checked by someone else for germs," Miss Twibell said. "She also visits all the patients to ask, without any of the staff in the room, how they're being treated. All except Mr. Farleigh."

"Why is he an exception?"

"I'll tell you that privately later," Miss Twibell said firmly.

"What else does she do?"

"She checks for dust and cobwebs. She examines the laundry that's been cleaned and ready to be used. She ascertains that anything that's been used on patients, like bandages or swabs, has been disposed of properly and promptly. She also looks for anything that might have been spilled and not cleaned up. She's very thorough. Chief Walker, you should talk to her. She'll tell you we've never had a single bad mark against us."

"I'll check with her even though I believe you. Why are your hands over your ears, Robert?"

Lily nudged him and repeated what Howard had asked.

"My ears are a bit cold," Robert lied. "I was just warming them up."

Howard was hard-pressed not to snort his disbelief. He knew what a sissy Robert was about other people's physical illnesses. Howard went on, "Who else was in Mr. Connor's room this morning?"

Betty was the one to respond. "His grandson Kelly. He came as Miss Quincy was leaving. He knows his grandmother always shows up on Monday or Tuesday at eleven in the morning, and Kelly comes to visit his grandfather earlier or later than she comes or on other days, when he's in town."

"Did he stay long?" Howard asked.

"No, I don't think so," Betty replied. "He brought some trinkets to him. I was out here in the main room. I glanced into Mr. Connor's room after Kelly left and they're still on the night table. Or they were then."

"Trinkets? What sort?" Howard asked.

"Oh, little samples of things. Chewing gum. Shaving brushes. Tiny tins of tooth powder and such," Betty replied.

"Don't any of you touch those things," Howard said. "I'll have to take them away for examination of the contents. How does this boy come to have these samples?"

This time Lily answered. "He drives an enclosed bus around to small towns in a couple counties that don't have drugstores. Towns like Voorburg. And goes house to house with samples. The whole containers are in the bus if you want to buy them."

"Where is he now? Does anybody know?"

Only Lily had a reply. "He was at Grace and Favor on Friday. I suppose he might still be nearby." There was a round of shrugs from the others. Even Miss Smith and Miss Jones, who usually were remarkably knowledgeable about people who visited the nursing home as well as many individuals who hadn't, garnered from the other women in their handwork group, had no good information.

The old ladies had taken in everything that had been asked or said, and were sure to inform their knitting-circle friends of every word, Miss Twibell thought. In fact, this was the only time she'd seen them awake and without knitting needles, crochet hooks, or yarn in their hands. She was wishing she'd imposed the same sanctions on them that the chief of police had made for the town reporter.

Howard asked Betty, "Did you check on Mr. Connor after this boy left?"

"Of course she did," Miss Twibell said.

Betty's face turned pink. "In fact, I didn't. I'd been up all night checking on him and fell asleep on the sofa out here. I didn't wake up until around a quarter of ten."

"I saw her sleeping when we got here a little after nine this morning," Lily said. "I tried not to disturb her."

"And at quarter of ten was she still sleeping?" Howard asked.

"I don't know. Robert and I were probably still taking the laundry downstairs by that time. I'm not wearing a watch today."

"Neither am I," Robert said.

"Did anyone else see the young man leave?"

"I was in my own room," Miss Twibell said. "Putting on real shoes before Mrs. Connor's visit."

"So were we. I mean, in our room," Miss Smith added.

"And when did Mrs. Connor arrive?" Howard asked.

"On the dot of eleven," Miss Twibell said. "You could set your watch by her arrival."

"What did she do first?"

"Walked into his room and started complaining that he was faking being asleep," Betty said. "Then she must have realized that the door was open and everybody could hear her and she slammed the door. But Miss Twibell and I could still faintly hear her spouting off at him about two of their farm workers quitting."

"And then . . . ?"

Miss Twibell said, "She burst out of the room and shouted that he wasn't breathing. Betty and I ran into the room to find out that she was right. She was still sobbing up a storm, so I took her out here and talked sense to her."

"What kind of sense?"

"That she needed to make funeral arrangements. That Dr. Polhemus had to sign the death certificate before Mr. Connor could be moved. She had to consult her husband's attorney, if he had one, about a will, and to see whether her husband had specified where he wanted to be buried. Then she pulled herself together and quit crying. I urged her to go and start this process. I wanted her to leave before the body was taken away. It's hard on a family member to see the body being wheeled off with a sheet over its face."

"Where were the rest of your patients and staff while this was going on?"

"I didn't really notice," Miss Twibell replied. "I think the Brewsters were in Miss Jones's and Miss Smith's room. I have no idea where Mr. Farleigh was. But probably outside. He's usually outdoors, except sometimes in the dead of winter when he's working in his greenhouse."

Howard rose from his chair and said, "That's all I need from you folks right now. I need to go to my car and get my envelopes to take away the trinkets. I need to try to find out where the grandson is now. I'll probably have to find a judge somewhere to order an autopsy, and someone to do it. I'll be back by at least tomorrow. Maybe sooner. Everybody," he said, looking around with a fierce Indian look that usually scared people, "think hard about what you saw and heard today, or even in the past, that might be relevant."

Howard headed back to his office at the jail, where he could place a long-distance call. His real office was at the boardinghouse, but there were too many alert, snoopy ears there. On his way, he dropped Jack off at the newspaper office with further warnings to keep what he'd heard at the nursing home confidential for the time being.

"You will keep in touch with me about the progress of

the case though, won't you? My promise will still hold until it's resolved," Jack said, and Howard agreed.

Once he reached the jailhouse, Howard consulted his list of phone numbers and rang the operator. Last November he had had cause to be in touch with the auditor in the state capital. He didn't need an audit this time, but thought this man might help him again. He warned the telephone exchange girl to hang up as soon as he was connected.

When the auditor answered the phone and he heard the click of the girl hanging up, Howard reminded him of their former conversations and said, "This time it's probably out of your realm, but you might be able to put me in touch with the right person."

"Glad to help if I can," the man replied.

"I have a body in a funeral parlor in Beacon. I'm sure it's murder. Even I recognize the signs. But I need an expert to examine him to confirm my view."

"Can't your own town provide a doctor who could do it?"

"Our town doctor's specialty is warts and gossip."

That made the man laugh out loud. "I see the problem. Let me make a few calls and see what I can find out. Call me back in three hours."

Howard added, "I'm sending a few product samples up to Albany as well. Could you arrange to have someone examine them to see that they're what they say they are on the label?"

"That's easy to do. Address the package to me and I'll see that it gets to the right person."

His next call was to the funeral home, warning the operator once again to hang up. He said to the owner of the home to do nothing to the body until he found an expert to examine it.

"We already know that it was suffocation. All the signs," he was told by the owner of the establishment.

"So do I. But neither of us is qualified to stand up in court and say so. I'll need someone who's officially an expert in cause of death to testify when I find out who did it. I might even have a judge look over the other evidence I have and let him order the process just to have it on the record."

"Okey-dokey. We've already put him on ice."

His next call was to his deputy, Ralph Summer. "Ralph, go up to the nursing home near Grace and Favor and ask Lily Brewster to describe the bus that Kelly Connor was driving. And then drive around Voorburg and see if you can find him. I understand his name is on the bus. Should be easy to spot."

Howard knew that Ralph would blab to his cousin Jack Summer, the town's newspaper editor. There was no helping that. He sighed and then proceeded to write down in a fresh notebook what everyone at the nursing home had said.

CHAPTER SIX

When Howard Walker called the auditor back, the man said, "I've found what you need. A good judge who's in Fishkill. And he knows a doctor who can do the autopsy. You'll need to bring the evidence and anyone who supports your view. I don't think from what you've said that it will be a problem. Oh, and he mentioned that he's an old friend of Mr. Prinney, your lawyer in Voorburg, so he'll come to Voorburg at ten tomorrow so that Prinney can sit in on the discussion."

Howard thanked him effusively, offering to return the favor anytime it was needed, and immediately called Miss Twibell. "We need to present the evidence at ten o'clock tomorrow to a judge from Fishkill who's coming up to Voorburg. I have the sheet and pillow in a paper bag. Bring Betty, and if you can locate this Miss Quincy, bring her along as well. I'll tell Dr. Polhemus he needs to be there, too. Lily and Robert Brewster can hold down the fort for an hour. It shouldn't take longer than that since it's so close."

Howard then cleared the plans with Mr. Prinney.

"I'd be glad to sit in," Mr. Prinney said. "I like Judge Grayson and haven't seen him for a long time. But let's get together at Grace and Favor. My office in town is too small for all these people plus the evidence. I'll bring my secretary along to take down what's said."

The only objection came from Robert. "Lily and I in charge of a nursing home? Dear God. What if one of them gets sick or croaks?"

"That's not likely in the hour it will take. Don't be such a sissy. If you can't cope, Lily will."

Tuesday morning at ten o'clock, they assembled in the dining room at Grace and Favor. Judge Grayson took a seat at one end of the table, Mr. Prinney at the other. Miss Twibell, Betty, and the visiting nurse sat on one side. Chief Walker, Mr. Waverly, who owned the funeral home, and Mr. Prinney's secretary, with her pen and shorthand pad, were on the other side of the table along with Dr. Polhemus.

Judge Grayson started by saying for the record, "This is a hearing conducted by Judge George Grayson on Tuesday, March seventh, 1933, in Voorburg-on-the-Hudson.

The hearing concerns the death of Mr. Sean Connor, a resident of Beacon, New York, who on March sixth died in Voorburg-on-Hudson."

Then he asked those who were present at the hearing to give their full names and their relationship to Mr. Sean Connor.

Judge Grayson looked at the evidence as Howard described what was on the pillowcase and the bottom sheet when it was discovered. The judge then asked Chief Walker a few questions about the events and their timing. Walker consulted his notes and read out what the witnesses had said. Judge Grayson then asked each of the witnesses if this was accurate to the best of their memories for the record. They all agreed.

He asked Miss Twibell, Miss Betty Stockton, and Miss Lucy Mae Quincy to each testify to Mr. Connor's condition when he entered the nursing home, his subsequent treatment, and his condition on the day he died.

Only Miss Quincy had anything to add. "When I was there, I checked that he really was in a coma. You can do this by running your knuckles fairly hard against the sternum. If they react to the pain, they're faking. He didn't react."

Next, Judge Grayson questioned Mr. Waverly. "Did you discover any other evidence of smothering when the body arrived at your funeral home?"

"His eyes had petechial hemorrhages," the man said.

"Would you describe what this means?"

"The whites of the eyes have spots of blood from the pressure on them."

Judge Grayson asked Dr. Polhemus, "Did you also notice this?"

"I'm afraid I didn't. I was just asked to pronounce him dead, which he obviously was. I had no reason to think it wasn't inevitable considering how he'd been in seriously failing health for the last several days."

Judge Grayson stared at Polhemus for a moment, then went on, "I don't think we need an inquest. Do you agree, Mr. Prinney?"

Mr. Prinney nodded. "The evidence seems quite clear and so does the testimony we've heard."

"If even the people at the funeral home recognize the signs of what happened, we can go straight to the autopsy," the judge said. "I know a good man for this. Chief Walker, do you want me to contact him?"

"If you would, please."

"Then my judgment is that Mr. Sean Connor was murdered by a person or persons unknown by means of smothering. This hearing is adjourned at 10:29 A.M. on the aforesaid day and further evidence will be sought by the chief of police of Voorburg-on-Hudson. The hearing is adjourned."

Everyone but Mr. Prinney and the judge left the room, but the two men stayed to have a long-delayed chat and catch up over cups of coffee and nutmeg-flavored cookies Mrs. Prinney had baked.

Lily and Robert were both relieved when Miss Twibell and Betty came back so quickly. Lily was eager to know how the hearing with the judge had gone, but didn't even have a chance to ask. Miss Twibell immediately asked for lunch to be prepared and served at the usual time and made a good pretense of this being like any other day. She complimented Lily on how well she'd cleaned the pharmacy during her absence, and asked Robert if he'd taken down all the laundry.

Lily realized Miss Twibell wasn't going to even refer to the hearing's having taken place. And Betty had probably been warned not to speak of it either.

Miss Twibell went to her room to change her shoes for her slippers, then came back.

"Are your feet feeling any better yet?" Lily asked.

"With all that's gone on recently, I almost forgot about them. Now I need you and Betty to get on with turning that mattress. We have a new patient coming in soon."

"This quickly?" Lily said with surprise.

"Yes, it's our own Mattie. Just as her mother thought Mattie was over the flu, the girl came down with pneumonia. Her mother's been worn out with all of her children feeling poorly. We can take part of the load off her. Mattie's mother has done a little nursing study herself and thinks it's a mild case, but would rather have her under our care. Now let's ready the room."

Betty led the way, bringing an extra chair along. "You sit down, Miss Twibell, and put your feet up and just supervise. Miss Brewster and I can handle this ourselves."

Under the sheets that had been taken away were two layers of white quiltlike padding that would have to go back to the laundry. The last layer over the mattress was some sort of heavy cloth that Lily thought must have been infused with paraffin to make it waterproof. It was very stiff, heavy, and hard to manage.

As they were untucking it to be cleaned in cold water and strong soap, Lily asked, "Miss Twibell, I'm wondering how you came to turn this house into a nursing home. If it's not too personal a question?"

"Not at all personal." Miss Twibell sat back comfortably. "But Betty will be bored. She's heard all this before.

"I'm the third generation to live in this house. I grew up here. I always wanted to be a nurse and my parents were moderately agreeable to the idea. Well-brought-up young women were supposed to marry and provide grandchildren. My parents thought getting a nursing degree was a good preparation for taking care of a brood of children. I'd been able to skip two grades in school, so I started nursing school at age sixteen. I soon discovered I really loved tak-

ing care of people. And would rather do that than marry,
so when I got my license after three years of study, I
applied to a hospital in New York City. After another three
years there, the Powers That Be decided I was such a good
nurse that I should be assigned to be head nurse in place of
the one who was retiring."

"What a compliment to your skills," Lily said.

"It was. The problem was that I didn't want the job. It
was more political and financial than medical. I would have
been in charge of hiring and firing nurses. I'd have to jus-
tify to the hospital board of directors what medicines
would be supplied and what they'd cost. I'd have been
responsible for how the scheduling of nursing shifts would
be set up. I'd lose all touch with the patients."

"So you turned down the offer?" Lily asked. "That
must have been a hard decision."

"Not really," Miss Twibell said cheerfully as she took
off one carpet slipper to massage her left foot. "I'd have
hated doing what they wanted me to do. It was flattering,
of course, but I'd have been miserable. Besides, my parents had need of me. They had me late in life and were
both in failing health. My father had suffered a stroke,
and my mother had cancer. So I came back here to take
care of them. I knew nursing. I knew, too, that I'd be doing
them their final favor for being so good to me. I also had
learned that I never wanted to be controlled by the whims
of a man. Being around so many middle-aged doctors

who mistook themselves for little gods had taught me that."

"Not all men are doctors," Lily said as she folded the stiff padding and put it into a laundry basket.

"All men are men, though," Miss Twibell said with a twinkle in her eye. "They want to be in charge of their family. Anyway, my father soon had his fatal stroke. My mother lingered for another two years. My father was the lucky one to go quickly. My mother was lonely for company when my father was gone, so I took in Miss Smith. She was already having trouble keeping up her house with her bad hips. She and my mother got along well with each other, listening to the radio and knitting. Miss Smith also liked me and offered me the annuity her father had purchased for her when she was a child as payment for keeping her and taking care of her for the rest of her life. It had built up over the years and supplied me with the extra money to set up all this"—she gestured at the main room and the pharmacy section—"after my mother passed away. That's how I managed to buy all the hospital beds, linens, pay for the shelving, and have these two rooms turned into one large one."

Lily and Betty perched on the edge of the now naked mattress.

Miss Twibell went on, "All Eulalia asked of me was free room and board and a small allowance to buy yarn," she chuckled. "Soon after that she introduced me to her friend

Miss Jones. They'd known each other all their lives. Miss Jones was fed up with living alone, and gave me title to sell her house in town with the same stipulation. Care and a small yarn allowance. And I'm not telling you tales I shouldn't reveal. Miss Smith and Miss Jones have told Betty, Mattie, and all their knitting-circle friends how happy they were with the bargain they made."

"I have one more snoopy question," Lily said. "How does a nurse manage to order all the medicines you must have to use?"

"That's not snoopy. It's a practical question. Dr. Polhemus orders it and I reimburse him for the cost. After all, my patients are his patients, too."

She put her carpet slipper back on and stood up. "Enough talking. You girls need to get this mattress turned and the bed put back together."

Just as she said this, Robert came huffing in with the last load of laundry for the day.

"Oh, dear. I completely forgot to warn you," she said to Lily and Robert, "yours is a seven-day-workweek job. But Doreen has the weekends off—that's why Friday is the heaviest washing day. Doreen needs Saturday and Sunday with her child. They go to their church on Sunday for a very long service. And for Sunday luncheon, Cook prepares trays of cold cuts and potato salad and cold cucumber soup that have to be brought up."

On their way home, Robert hadn't even started the

automobile before beginning to complain. Lily held her hand up to stop him.

"We'll make more money this way. Keep that in mind. And it's not as if we have parties to go to on weekends anyway. Besides all that, Doreen works far harder than we do in that steamy room in the basement. We carry *dry* linens up and down. She has to wrestle with them waterlogged and hot, get them starched and dried, then work with a hot iron."

Robert hated to admit she was right, so he just shrugged.

CHAPTER SEVEN

Tuesday evening, while Robert sat in the library trying to find some news on the radio, and Lily was reading a new mystery novel that Miss Exley, the town librarian, had ordered specifically for her, Lily asked Robert, "Who do you think smothered that old man?"

"Huh? What old . . . ? Oh, Mr. Connor? It could have been anyone who lives or works there except us, and the Smith and Jones ladies."

"Probably not anyone, exactly," Lily said. "Doreen never comes upstairs. Neither does the cook. At least we've never seen her."

"The cook sends the vegetable-peeler-and-washer-upper girl up though," he said in a teasing voice.

"Robert, aren't you curious?"

"Not especially. Everybody seemed to know he didn't have much time to live anyway."

"But that's exactly what's so odd about it," Lily said.

"Why risk smothering an old man who is going to die within a matter of a few hours anyway?"

She finally had Robert's attention. He turned the radio off and said, "That's a good question. My money's on Betty."

"Oh, no. She's such a nice girl."

"You're overlooking the fact that she was his primary tormentor. Messing about all the time with his knee, which must have been really painful before he went comatose. He probably was really mean and hateful to her."

"I'll admit that," Lily said. "But not at the end. He couldn't react to anything that was done to him. Why would she bother killing him on his last day of life? And he was a small, feeble old man. Anybody could have probably smothered him earlier. The visiting nurse, or that grandson. Or maybe even someone who sneaked in when nobody was looking. And there are times nobody is in that big living room. Anybody from outside the house could have come in."

Robert ignored almost everything she said, but commented, "Sometimes the little wiry old men are a lot stronger than they look."

"Still, I don't think it was Betty," Lily said.

"What about Miss Twibell then? She must have a long waiting list of people needing to fill that bed. Maybe some of them were really rich."

"That's nonsense!" Lily nearly yelped. "She's too

proud of her perfect record to take the chance, knowing he had only hours to live."

"Okay. I agree. So who else could have done it?"

"The last person in his room, of course. His wife," Lily said.

"Not if it's true that she was there to ask his help to find new workers. Wasn't that what we were told she was yelling at him about?" Robert asked.

"Maybe she simply got fed up with him pretending to be in deep sleep when she was there," Lily argued.

Robert turned the radio back on. "It's not our problem. It's Howard's job and he's good at it."

"But we've usually been of some help to him with previous cases."

"Because we butted in," Robert said with a laugh. "He never really asked us to help."

"Yes, he did," Lily objected. "Remember when he wanted you to go with him to interview that tailor in New York? When you found a body in the old icehouse? And he asked me to go along last November when he was interviewing several young women."

"That's only because he doesn't have a woman assistant in the department, and wanted a witness to the fact that he wasn't up to any hanky-panky if any of those young women complained to the officials."

Lily's eyes lit up. "Maybe I could train to be a policewoman!"

Robert's laugh this time was nearly a bark. "Lily! Get away. You just want to hang around Walker. I don't blame you. He's a good-looking man. But he's as poor as we are."

Lily was indignant. "You dare think I want to marry Howard? That's an outrageous thing to say."

"You'll marry someone someday," Robert said, further goading her.

"Robert, look how many spinsters and widows just in Voorburg make their own way. Roxanne Anderson. Mrs. Tarkington. Miss Jurgen. And I'll bet that young woman who is the visiting nurse is single, too."

"There's no shortage of bachelors either, Lily. Howard Walker, the Harbinger boys, Jack and Ralph Summer. They're all doing fine, too. And so am I."

Lily shuddered at the idea of anyone having Ralph as a husband. Ralph was a lout.

She said, "Hmm. Maybe I could train as a matchmaker instead of a policewoman." She took her mystery and stomped upstairs to her room. She was irritated with Robert for taking no interest in Mr. Connor's death and for teasing her about Howard. But she found herself unable to concentrate on her book.

It was bizarre that anyone would have a motive for killing a man who was certainly going to die anyway within the day. Who would need to do that? Whatever the mean old man had done to someone, he clearly couldn't ever do it again.

On the other hand, Robert might have made a better argument for Betty or Miss Twibell having done the deed. Both of them, in a desperate effort to save Mr. Connor's life, were clearly inflicting pain on him by cleaning the wound. This was their job and it probably made him angry and even meaner. Could he have tried to attack one or the other of them to make them stop? Perhaps repeatedly? Miss Twibell was larger and stronger in mind and body than Betty, who was young. Could one of them have taken revenge on him for something he'd said or done to her?

Lily couldn't picture Betty as the murderer, because Betty was nice girl and a workhorse. But it was possible. Lily didn't know her well enough to judge.

She was certain, however, that Miss Twibell, who was so proud of what she did, taking excellent care of the infirm and dotty, wouldn't have taken the risk. She, better than anyone else, recognized that he was doomed to die that day. In spite of Robert's theory, which was probably thought up to annoy Lily, Miss Twibell ran a tight ship. And Lily knew for sure that neither Miss Smith nor Miss Jones had the strength or the endurance to have smothered the old man.

Then there was the mysterious gardener, Mr. Farleigh. Miss Twibell had been very wary of saying anything at all about him except that he was often outdoors. Did anyone else who was a patient know anything about him? Even Miss Jones and Miss Smith hadn't gossiped about him.

But then, she hadn't asked them their opinion. She might have to do that.

She gave a brief thought to Doreen and immediately dismissed her as a suspect. She had to be strong enough to smother him, doing all that heavy work with the laundry. But as far as Lily knew, she didn't come upstairs and probably didn't even know the patients. The same thing applied to the cook and the skivvy, she assumed. What could either of them have had against Mr. Connor? What did they stand to gain from his death? She couldn't imagine an answer to either question.

Was there any tactful way to question Miss Twibell about her patients? Lily didn't think she could or should do it, in spite of her curious nature. And Robert had been right about one thing. It was Chief of Police Howard Walker's job to ask the questions.

She tried hard to put her own questions out of her mind and read her book. Fictional murder was harmless and rather silly sometimes. The real thing could be dangerous at the hands of snoops, as she'd learned.

But there was always a chance to eavesdrop.

Howard Walker wasn't surprised when Jack Summer called on him at the boardinghouse that evening.

"I hear by the grapevine that there was a meeting at Grace and Favor."

"That's true. A judge has ruled that the old man was murdered by a person or persons unknown."

"What else can you tell me? I should probably write up an obituary."

"I question that. He wasn't from Voorburg. The Beacon newspaper will do that."

"Could I interview the widow?" Jack asked.

"If you want to. But she's a big tough woman you're not going to like."

"Then what can I say in the paper?"

"Just what I told you officially. A man named Sean Connor, from Beacon, died under suspicious circumstances in Voorburg. And don't mention the nursing home. Miss Twibell has an excellent reputation for caring for her patients and doesn't deserve to be implicated."

Jack was naturally disappointed with such meager information. But he'd keep his ear to the ground anyway. This might turn into a good story for his newspaper eventually.

Wednesday morning, Lily did, in fact, hear some gossip. And without even meaning to. At first.

Betty had already cleaned the floor and counter of the

pharmacy part of the big room. She was free of Mr. Connor at last and could get back to her usual work. But Robert, who could flirt the spots off pigs, had persuaded her to accompany him downstairs with the laundry to visit with Doreen and her little boy, Buddy.

"You can tidy up the storeroom if you're looking for something to do," Betty tossed over her shoulder to Lily as she followed Robert with a small basket of linens.

The storeroom door was off to the right of the locked shelves of medications. It really had become untidy. There were mops and brooms and what Lily thought of as "scooper-uppers," though Mimi would surely know the right name for these objects. Then she remembered hearing Mimi call them dustpans.

There was a wastebasket full of newspapers, old tattered magazines, and a wealth of little scraps of yarn. She'd have to ask later what to do with that. Looking up at the shelves, she realized they weren't as well organized as they might be. The floor polish sat next to a bottle of peroxide. The dust rags were as far as they could be from the lemon oil.

As she was plotting out how to rearrange things, she heard voices. Miss Twibell was talking quietly to Chief Walker.

"Why didn't you want to talk to me about Mark Farleigh?" he asked.

"I don't like revealing any of my patients' ailments,"

she said. "If they want to talk about them to their friends, or you, or me, that's all right. But I don't pass it on to anyone but those authorized to know. The visiting nurse and Dr. Polhemus."

"And the law," Howard said softly. "That, too, is 'authority' in spite of your scruples, which I do understand. I need to know about everyone. And won't ever reveal anything that isn't absolutely necessary to this case."

Miss Twibell was silent for a moment. "I think I must trust you to keep that promise."

CHAPTER EIGHT

There was another long silence while Miss Twibell apparently decided how much to tell Walker. Lily froze in place.

"Mark Farleigh," Walker reminded her. "I've never even seen him except outside. Is he a patient or an employee?"

"He's both," Miss Twibell said. "He was a young man studying to be a botanist before the Great War. Frankly, I think he signed up to serve just so that he'd have a chance of seeing plants in France that might not grow here. But that's just a guess."

"Shell shock?" Walker asked.

Miss Twibell said, "Yes, the worst kind. The silent kind. He wouldn't even talk to his parents when he came home from the war—thin and looking ten years older than he was a year and half earlier. They were frankly embarrassed by having a grown son at home who apparently couldn't or wouldn't speak. They were in the habit of having parties back in those days before the Crash in '29, and their guests were always asking where their heroic son was."

"How did you become involved?"

"They didn't want to take him to Dr. Polhemus. He's a gossip."

"Don't we *all* know that? I can't tell you how many people he's told about the newspaper editor's warts."

"He doesn't gossip about my patients though," she said. "I made him swear on his mother's grave that he'd never speak to anyone else about them. And, surprisingly, he seems to have kept his promise. Anyway, that's why Mark's parents brought him to me. They wanted to tell their friends that Mark had taken a job in a distant city. When, in fact, they live barely ten miles away."

Lily was supposed to be tidying the storeroom, but now she had to do so in complete silence as she continued to listen.

"They offered to pay you to keep him here?" Walker asked her.

"They offered. But it was a stingy offer. And in all fairness, they might not have been able to afford much more. And there were no more payments after the Crash. They must have lost their money like most people did. But I took a liking to Mark the first time I saw him, and it didn't matter by then.

"When they brought him here, there was a flower

arrangement on the table right in front of us, and he stared at it with a faint smile the whole time the family was here," she went on. "I thought that slight smile was a good sign."

"So you kept him on? How long has he been here?"

"Since I came home to take care of my mother in her final years. That was in late 1923, and the grounds hadn't been cared for in years. It was a jungle out there. I thought if he liked flowers, he could occupy himself in the yard."

"And that worked out?"

"Wonderfully. His parents took him to the front door to say their goodbyes, and when the door had closed, he turned to me and said, "Your yard is a mess. I'll fix it."

Lily almost gave herself away with a gasp of surprise.

"He really *could* talk?" Walker asked.

"He can. But he doesn't like to. He seldom comes into this room and when he does it's only for special occasions like birthday parties for the old ladies. Then he just sits and smiles. They think he's a mute. He spends most of his time outside. There's a little shed on the grounds behind the pines that has heat and light. He spends most of his time out there, even in the dead of winter. And in the spring and summer, he creeps in here and sets out lovely flower arrangements. Even Miss Jones and Miss Smith haven't figured out where they come from. I tell them it's from a secret admirer of mine," she said with a girlish giggle.

"Does Mr. Farleigh still talk to you?"

"Not often. But my suite of rooms are close to his. I've often heard him crying in the middle of the night. Not loudly and not for long. He gets up and dresses and goes to the shed to recover. I'm allowed to talk to him, however. And when I ask him to take on some project or another, he agrees and says, 'I'll start it right now.' And if I compliment him on his work, he thanks me."

With a smile in her voice, she continued, "One time, three years ago, I asked him what we should do about a part of the backyard that was eroding, and he just said he'd take care of it. He spent the whole summer building the most magnificent brick wall you'll ever see. And to this day, I don't know how or where he got the bricks. He also added a heated greenhouse to the south side of the shed to grow flowers in the winter, and pot up seeds for spring plantings. He must have foraged the glass from the town dump."

Howard laughed, then asked, "Do his parents visit him?"

"They did at first. But it just set him back. I advised them to just write to him if they wanted. And every month I write to them, telling them what projects he's working on. They never reply to me, nor does he reply to them, as far as I know."

"Did he ever come in contact with Mr. Connor?"

"I know he didn't," Miss Twibell said. "The first day Sean Connor was here, he started shouting orders at everyone. What he didn't like to eat. How rough the sheets felt. Trying to get me to go out and buy him whiskey. I saw

Mark almost come through the door to this room, but when he heard Mr. Connor's tirade he fled. He hasn't been back here since that day three months ago."

"You're sure his . . . well, mental and emotional condition isn't abnormal?" Walker asked.

"Absolutely certain. I'd stake my own life on that. He's the least dangerous person I've ever known."

There was such a note of finality to this that Lily backed out the storeroom door, dragging the heavy waste bin. She turned and said, "Oh, I didn't know anyone was out here. Miss Twibell, where can I empty this? I've been sorting things out. . . ."

"Just take it into the hallway and I'll have it taken care of. Thanks for tidying up in there. I was planning to do it myself this afternoon. Where are Robert and Betty, do you know?"

"They went down with the laundry a while ago."

Miss Twibell opened the door to the hall and went on her way to fetch them back via the bell system in her room, and Howard relieved Lily of the heavy waste bin, took it to the hall, and then came back into the living room.

"You heard every word of that conversation, didn't you?" he said with dangerous blandness.

Lily felt her face get hot. "I did. But I promise you I'll never tell." She was so embarrassed, she knew she meant it. She'd have loved to tell Robert what she'd heard. She never would though.

When Miss Twibell, now wearing her carpet slippers again, came back from summoning Robert and Betty, she said to Howard that she had to get back to work, but he could come back tomorrow if need be. When he'd left, she took a look at the storeroom.

"You did a good job of this. It's amazing how things slip when one of my regular employees is gone and I'm not in top form myself. Thanks for taking this on, Miss Brewster."

"Are your feet feeling better?" Lily asked.

"Not much. I had almost forgotten about them. It's only now that I realize they do still hurt."

Betty returned and was apologetic. "I'm sorry, Miss Twibell. I was playing with Buddy while Mr. Brewster was chatting with Doreen."

"A little bit less of playing and chatting might be a good idea," Miss Twibell said mildly. "Now we need to get on with our work."

CHAPTER NINE

Thursday turned out to be the easiest day Lily and Robert had had yet. There was no laundry to haul up and down. And Betty had already washed the shelves of the pharmacy part of the room. Lily insisted on doing the two mop-ups. "You still look tired. You need to rest," Lily told her.

Robert was reading the paper, reclining on the sofa with his shoes off so he wouldn't get the arm of it dirty. "Looks like the banks are going to be closed longer than we thought," he said as Lily mopped.

When she said "Oh?" without much interest, he went on, "It seemed to me from the start that five days was too short a time to get all the changes in the laws of banking drawn up and approved."

Lily doubted that he'd thought this out on the day the banks closed. It must have been what he'd just read.

She finished the mopping and drying and sat down on

one of the side chairs. It was so peaceful today. And they were being paid for reading the paper and sitting around. She felt guilty about it. But not too guilty. They'd both put in a lot of hard work on the previous days.

Robert set aside the paper and they both politely stood up when Miss Twibell entered the room. At least their expensive educations had drilled good manners into them. Nothing else they'd learned then had prepared them for the life they were now leading.

"Miss Brewster, would you mind going downstairs with your brother to wait for Mattie to arrive? It's not fair to Doreen to have to leave her work to be alert to visitors at the door when she already has so much work to do. Mr. Brewster, Mattie is a strong-minded girl. She'll want to walk up the stairs. I leave it to you to carry her up if, in your judgment, she's too weak to do so."

This was clearly an order but she said it so politely and gently that it wasn't the least offensive.

As they headed out the door, Miss Twibell said, "Mr. Brewster? Your shoes?"

Robert looked down at his stockinged feet and laughed as he put them back on.

He resumed chuckling as they descended.

"What's so funny?" Lily asked.

"You. I'd bet good money you're still trying to find a tactful way to find out what happened at that hearing on Tuesday. You're not going to get a word out of Betty or

Miss Twibell, and I'll bet Mr. Prinney will zip his lip as well. There's no point in trying to pry it out of anyone who was there."

"I'm afraid you're right. I've already given up the idea. But consider this: they were back so quickly that it must have gone well. If there had been a division of opinion, it would have taken much longer."

A car pulled up close to the front door and both of them went to help Mattie in. But it was her father bringing her. He was a big strong man who lifted her in his arms and carried her to the door.

"I'm Mattie's dad. Who are you two?" he said as they followed him up the stairs.

"We're Mattie's temporary substitutes. We've decided it takes two of us to replace her," Lily replied and gave him their names, adding, "Are you sure you don't need my brother's help?"

"Nope. She ain't that heavy. She's lost weight what with being so sickly."

Miss Twibell was at the head of the stairs to greet them. "Thank you, Mr. Rockwell, for bringing Mattie back to us, even if she is a patient for a change. Come in and sit down while we put her to bed and examine her. You can then stay and have lunch in her room with her."

Her father set her down. She looked pale and a little wobbly, but with Miss Twibell holding one elbow and

Betty holding the other, they got her into her room and closed the door.

Miss Smith, maneuvering on her pair of canes, followed by Miss Jones, came out of their room to greet him. "It's good to meet you again, Mr. Rockwell. We haven't seen you for a long time. We're so sorry that Mattie's ill."

He'd stood as they approached, and then helped Miss Smith get comfortably into one of the chairs and set her sticks where she could reach them easily.

When both ladies were seated, he said, "She ain't all that sick, just a bit weak. It's really that my wife is about to fall apart takin' care of a houseful of our other puny kids. Mattie likes it here, and we know Miss Twibell will take good care of her."

Lunch came along shortly and both the kitchen girl and the cook herself brought up big covered trays and set them down on the table in front of the sofa. "We got another two to bring up," the cook said as they disappeared.

Miss Twibell came out of Mattie's room and lifted one of the lids. There were two plates under it. "Warmed-up leftover pot roast sandwiches from dinner last night. I think it's always better the second time. And some nice fried potatoes."

She sat down on the sofa and said, "Mr. Rockwell, your daughter's going to be fine. She only has a very slight temperature; her lungs sound good. Her heartbeat is good. She only needs to get a lot of quiet sleep and come back to eating more and she'll be fine in a few days. Go on in to see her and someone will bring your lunches," she said, glancing at Robert and Lily.

Lily pushed the door open with her elbow and set Mattie's plate down on a tray on Mattie's lap. Mattie already looked a little better—not so pale. Lily couldn't help but notice that Mattie's arms, revealed by her short-sleeved hospital gown, were well muscled. That must have come from hauling all that laundry up and down.

Robert followed with another plate, which he handed to her father while he pulled one of the nightstands over to serve as a table, and said, "We'll be right back with silverware and drinks."

They returned with a big glass of milk for Mattie and a small glass of beer for her father. A little vase of fresh grape hyacinths was sitting on the windowsill, and Lily set it on Mattie's tray. "Mr. Farleigh must have put these here for you," Lily said.

Mattie smiled and raised the vase to her nose. "They smell like spring rain."

As Robert closed the door behind them, the cook and her skivvy were already back, passing out plates, cutlery, coffee, and tea to Miss Twibell, Miss Smith, and Miss Jones, who had chosen to eat right where they were, off the little side tables. "Be back with the rest shortly."

The rest of the afternoon passed quietly. Betty helped

Lily with the afternoon cleaning of the pharmacy area, and Lily later joined Robert as he carried down a small basket of laundry. The laundry area was deserted but they could hear Buddy laughing.

There was a large window facing the backyard, and they went to look. Doreen had her back to them and was wearing a big heavy shawl that Lily could tell by the vivid colors was one either Miss Smith or Miss Jones had made for her.

Buddy was on a teeter-totter and Mr. Farleigh was on the other end of it. He wasn't laughing, but he was smiling.

"I'd like to have a picture of this," Lily said sappily.

"Have you learned anything about him?" Robert asked. "Whether he's a patient or an employee?"

"Not a thing," Lily lied. She hated to fib to Robert, but a promise was a promise for all time.

Later in the afternoon, once the plates were cleared, Lily had the leisure to get to read a few of the women's magazines that were back on the big table in front of the sofa. Robert entertained the old ladies, then took a short nap in one of the chairs and didn't even snore.

When Miss Twibell came back into the living room, Lily took her aside and said, "Robert made what might be a good suggestion I thought I should tell you. He thinks it might be a good idea to put in a dumbwaiter that goes between this floor and the basement."

"Hmm. That might work. It would save the cook the

trouble of bringing the trays up, and Mattie and Betty having to haul the baskets of linens. I wonder how big it would have to be and what it would cost."

"Robert could ask the Harbinger brothers to come out and measure this floor, the ground floor, and the basement and see if there's a way to do it. And you can ask them to give you a bid. We've hired them before. They're good strong workers and don't overcharge."

"Do ask Robert to ask them to come around tomorrow if they can. I hope it can work out."

CHAPTER TEN

On Friday Miss Twibell told Robert that Lily had told her about his dumbwaiter suggestion and that she thought it was something worth investigating. Robert thought how much easier it would be to just roll laundry baskets and trays of food into a closet and send things whichever way they needed to be sent. This was in spite of the fact that he devoutly hoped he wouldn't still be working here to enjoy the benefit, hoped he'd be remembered as the person who had had such a brilliant time- and effort-saving idea.

He called the Harbinger house and was told by Mrs. Harbinger that Harry was just finishing up repairing a lock and asked if he could call back.

Robert asked her to tell Harry to call him back at the nursing home.

"You're not hurt or sick, are you?" Mrs. Harbinger said with alarm.

"No, I'm not. My sister and I are just filling in for a sick nurse."

Harry called back in ten minutes. "Mom was worried about you. What do you need?"

Robert explained what a dumbwaiter was and approximately how he thought it worked, not that he'd ever actually used one of them.

"Ropes and pulleys," Harry said. "Easy if there's room to do it at each floor at the same place above and below."

"Have you ever built one?"

"No. But my folks took us to New York once and there was a big store that had them. I wanted to see how they worked and Dad made somebody show me."

"Good enough. Miss Twibell is interested in having you see if it's possible and how much it would cost."

"Give me directions to this place, and I'll bring my brother along to write down dimensions," Harry said.

"You mean right now?"

"Nobody much wants us working at their houses on Fridays. They're afraid we'll leave a mess they'll be tripping over all weekend. We finished one job yesterday and don't have anything else lined up yet. We'll be there in a tick."

Robert waited anxiously, wondering what was taking them so long. When he passed a window, he saw that they were already outside and measuring the dimensions of the entire house. This was an obvious way to start, he realized, feeling quite silly not to have realized it until he saw them.

A little while later, they knocked at the door and Robert rushed to let them in. Harry had a big paper with grid lines. The outside dimensions were all written down at the edges.

"Where do you want to start?" Robert asked. "On the second floor or the basement?"

"The ground floor," Harry said. "We don't want to run it down through the middle of a dining room or a parlor."

As they started taking measurements, Robert went back upstairs to ask Miss Twibell's permission to help them. But he had to wait for a while. Miss Twibell was busy telling Mattie she was welcome to come out and sit in the living room, but she absolutely *wasn't* allowed to make her bed first. "You aren't working here, my dear child. You are a patient who needs all the rest you can get. No more of this, understand?"

Mattie wasn't offended by this edict. She smiled and said, "I've made so many beds here that I just did so without even thinking about it."

Miss Twibell led Mattie to the sofa, then brought her a pillow and a nice wool throw.

As Miss Twibell sat down in one of the side chairs, Robert asked if he could help Harry and Jim do the measurements.

"They're already here?" she said with surprise.

Three hours later, Robert and the Harbinger boys came up to the second floor. Robert looked smug. Harry asked Miss Twibell if he could look in the storeroom to take his last measurements.

"Of course. I'd hate to lose the storeroom though. It's so handy."

The three young men didn't say anything as they went into the storeroom. They'd closed the door and Miss Twibell, Lily, and Betty crept closer to see if they could hear through it.

Mattie had already been fed lunch and put back into bed for a nap. The door to the Smith and Jones room opened and the ladies came out. "What's that noise behind our wall?" Miss Smith asked eagerly. "Is something interesting going on?"

"It might be interesting. We're waiting to hear," Lily told her. "Why don't you ladies sit down and try to guess what's happening?"

Robert and the Harbinger boys came out, smiling and slapping each other on the back.

"It can be done, Miss Twibell," Harry Harbinger said. "If you could clear that table in front of the sofa, I'll show you how."

When the magazines, newspapers, and flowers had all

been removed, everybody moved closer to look at the sheet showing the second floor. Harry said, "My brother and I will be back tomorrow to double-check our measurements, but as they read now, the dumbwaiter can go in right behind the door to that storeroom."

"How will we get past it?" Miss Twibell asked.

Harry looked at her a brief moment and said, without any hint of criticism of her degree of common sense, "We move the door to the other side of the storeroom. Then move the shelving to the right end of the wall. You'll still have almost as much room in there, especially if we put hooks on the wall to hang brooms, mops, and buckets."

Miss Twibell had the grace to say, "What a fool question to ask. I should have thought of it."

Harry smiled and said, rolling out another big sheet of gridded paper, "This shows the ground floor. I'm putting it down exactly on top of the map of this floor and have marked where the shaft will go. You'll lose your smallest bathroom, but there is another, larger one on that floor already. Are you willing to do that?"

"I don't think anyone's used that little bathroom for years. Yes, if it's necessary, I wouldn't mind."

Now Harry flourished the third sheet with a flare of victory. "See where it comes out in the basement?"

Miss Twibell, Betty, Lily, and the Misses Smith and Jones leaned even closer.

Betty crowed, "Right between the laundry room and the kitchen!"

"Ain't that lucky?" Jim Harbinger said. "Neat as a pin. We was over the moon when we caught on."

"Could the opening be on both sides?" Miss Twibell asked. She was finally sounding genuinely excited now that she understood what they were planning.

"Yes," Harry said. "It isn't a load-bearing wall. It looks like it was added after the house was built."

Miss Twibell sat back in her chair, no longer smiling. "Now give me the bad news. What will it cost to do this?"

Jim opened his mouth to speak, but Harry, by far the smarter and more sensible of the brothers, poked him lightly in the ribs and wrote a figure down on a slip of paper and passed it to her. He always worked on the assumption that only the person or a married couple paying for the work needed to know the cost.

Miss Twibell read the number and she had to fight to keep her chin from dropping. It was half what she feared it would cost.

Before she could reply, Harry went on, "Now, if you want to electrify it, that will cost another ten dollars."

"What happens if the power goes out in a storm?" Lily asked.

"You'd still have the ropes and the drum they roll around to pull it up or lower it. If it's a heavy load, it might take a lot of muscle to do that. Since it appears that most of the work here is done by ladies, I think you should run it with electricity. We'll see if it's needed when the work is done. You might be able to do it with just the ropes."

"When can you start?" Miss Twibell asked.

"Day after tomorrow if you will be ready," Harry said. "We need to measure again to make sure we did it right, and then go to Poughkeepsie to get the materials to do it. If you don't mind us working here on Sunday."

Miss Twibell turned to Robert and said, "Thank you so much for thinking of this and knowing the right men to do it."

"It's only because I'm lazy," Robert admitted.

Chief Walker returned to the nursing home Friday after-noon. Jack Summer had been to his office at the jail earlier, asking about the sample products Walker had taken away.

"They were all perfectly innocent. I felt a bit of an ass for asking to have them examined. So please don't ever mention it when you're free to write about this."

When Walker arrived on the second floor of the nursing home, the big room and hallway outside were chaotic. Bottles, mops, boxes of swabs, buckets, and things he couldn't even identify were being carried out to the vacant room down the hallway. Miss Twibell, Betty, Lily, and Robert were too busy to even notice at first that he was there.

As Miss Twibell came back empty-handed, Walker asked, "Does this have anything to with the Harbinger boys' pickup truck being parked in your drive?"

"Oh, Chief Walker, I'm sorry. I didn't know you were here. Yes, the young men are here to double-check the measurements they made this morning. We're putting a dumbwaiter from the basement to this floor. It was Mr. Brewster's suggestion."

"It would be," Walker said with a smile. "Could you possibly let the others tend to this for a while? I need to ask you some questions."

"I'd rather supervise the move to the extra guest room. Do you have many questions or just a few?"

"I'll start with the first one and ask the others when you're finished."

Miss Twibell looked around the room. Miss Jones and Miss Smith were settled in their chairs in the living room, enjoying watching everyone else haul things out. Mattie had even been allowed out of her room to watch as well.

"We'll go to my suite then," Miss Twibell said, leading him there.

They sat down in the chairs facing the back window. They could see the Harbinger boys outside taking their measurements again. Mr. Farleigh was also out there picking a few daffodils that were still in bud. Jim Harbinger called out to Farleigh, "Pretty flowers." Farleigh smiled and held them up for Jim to see, and went back to cutting a few more.

Miss Twibell tapped Walker lightly on the knee and asked, "What is the question?"

"I'm sorry. That was a nice exchange of greetings. The first question is, how many visitors have you had here since Mr. Connor first arrived?"

CHAPTER ELEVEN

"That's a bigger question than I anticipated," Miss Twibell said sourly. "We have many visitors. Too many sometimes. The ladies from Miss Jones's and Miss Smith's hold their knitting and crocheting meeting once a week in the living room, unless we have a crisis going on and they're in the way. Then they cram themselves into the Smith and Jones room. I couldn't even tell you all their names or which of the group came which week."

"Are they all older women?"

"No, as the old ones die out or members move away, they take in younger women. What is the relevance of this?"

He knew some of the older ladies might have had a serious grudge against Sean Connor but probably didn't have the strength necessary to smother him. The younger ones might have been able to if they had some obscure reason to want to.

He only replied, "I don't know yet what is important to know. Who else has visited?"

She was growing more irritable. "Mrs. Connor, of course. Early on in his stay, a few of his neighboring farmers visited. I can't imagine it was out of affection. Just a sense of duty. Their wives probably insisted it was the neighborly thing to do. And I don't know their names either."

She went on, "Another man who didn't introduce himself, and was closeted with Mr. Connor for nearly an hour, was here several weeks ago. He must have been a lawyer. He had a bulging leather case with him, and before he left, he asked Betty and me to sign the back of a sheet of paper as witnesses after Mr. Connor signed it. A deed or something."

"Anyone else?" Walker knew he was trying her patience, but needed any information he could get as soon as he could.

"We had a handsome young man in what I call the 'overflow' room for a while because he'd wrenched his back badly falling off a tractor. He needed constant changing of hot packs alternating with cold packs and had no close family to help. He was a patient for only five days and had a whole string of pretty young girls visit. If I think of anyone else, I'll let you know. I really must get back to work."

"One more really easy question I must ask," Howard plowed on. "Is the front door always locked?"

"Not necessarily. Generally, we keep it locked. But when we're expecting someone like the Harbinger brothers, Mrs. Connor, or Dr. Polhemus, it's unlocked."

With that she swept out of the room, walking hard on her heels.

She'd left so abruptly that Walker hadn't even had time to perform the courtesy of standing up when she did. He remained sullenly seated when she had departed. The answer to the front door question had set him back. It wasn't the reply he'd anticipated, and not an answer he liked.

Anyone could have walked in when the assistants were taking down laundry, Miss Smith and Miss Jones were in their room, and Miss Twibell was in her suite. Theoretically there must have been several times that almost anybody could have arrived and departed without any of the staff or patients knowing about it.

Perhaps even the very morning Connor died. They'd expected Mrs. Connor to arrive, but not until eleven in the morning. The visiting nurse who arrived so early might have warned them the day before that she was coming and the door might have been unlocked for her sake. Could someone have slipped in overnight and hidden until the coast was clear? Maybe peeking through the door of what Miss Twibell had called the "overflow room" to see when all the regulars were gone? But who, outside the patients and staff, would know who the regulars were?

He'd made Miss Twibell impatient and didn't dare to question her again when she was busy. That could take quite a while during the construction of this dumbwaiter.

He might as well go to the storeroom and pitch in and help cart boxes. It might move the process along a little bit faster.

Miss Twibell stopped glaring at Chief Walker when he said, "Here, Robert, let's get the last of these things put away so we can take down the glass doors and put them somewhere safe."

"How do you remove them?" Robert asked.

Walker showed him how easy it was after the last of the flasks, pestles, and measuring cups and spoons had been put into a box and stored in the overflow room.

Miss Twibell finally stopped giving directions and sat down on the sofa. Miss Smith and Miss Jones were still watching all this activity avidly. Lily, having taken the last box to the overflow room, leaned on the arm of the sofa, commenting on what a pleasure it was to sit and watch men working.

When the glass doors and the old door to the storeroom had all been removed, Robert, thrilled to have discovered a new set of skills, said, "Now let's take out the cabinets and counter, shall we?"

"I'm not so sure of that," Walker admitted. "I've never done it. I think we'll leave that to the Harbinger boys. They'd have done what we've accomplished in a third of the time it took us. But I'm sure they'd let you watch. Maybe even help with supporting the cabinets while they remove whatever is holding them up."

He'd shown Robert how to remove doors. But he knew his own limits. Trying to get a big heavy cabinet down intact was way beyond him and surely something Robert wouldn't know about.

When Walker and Robert gave up, the spectators did as well. Miss Twibell went to check Mattie's temperature. Lily and Betty swept up the debris that had accumulated around the work site. They had a hard time finding where someone had put the dustpan.

Robert said as he picked up one of the big baskets of laundry, "Just think. In a few days nobody will ever have to do this again."

Walker helped Miss Smith to her feet and escorted her and Miss Jones back to their room. After they picked up their yarn and knitting needles, they asked if he could stay a while and visit with them. Miss Smith offered him some caramels. He had to turn them down. He didn't want his teeth stuck in them when he intended to question them, but he did accept a peppermint lozenge, which he could crunch up and swallow quickly.

"I understand you hold knitting parties here every week."

"Well, almost every week. If another patient is seriously ill, like Mr. Connor was at the end, it's usually held somewhere else and we miss it. If it's a small group of two or three, we all sit in here," Miss Smith said.

He looked at the finished, folded work on the far wall. "You give these away to people who need them?" he asked. "How do you do that?"

"Mrs. White brings that dear second husband of hers to help take them to the three churches in town to give to anybody who asks."

"Sometimes they just drive house to house with them, offering them," Miss Jones added, somewhat breathlessly.

"She's the pillar of Voorburg," Miss Smith said.

Howard nodded. He didn't necessarily agree entirely with that. He thought a number of people in Voorburg also deserved praise: Mrs. Tarkington, the school principal; Jack Summer, who was the editor of the best newspaper in the county; Mr. and Mrs. Prinney.

Maybe even himself.

Walker let a few silent moments pass, trying to figure out a way to change the subject to the Connor family. He needn't have bothered. Miss Smith said, "Do you know about the Connor family history?"

"Not a thing. I'd never heard of any of them until Mr. Connor died," Walker replied.

Miss Smith launched into the same story she'd told Robert. How Mr. Connor and his son had a big blowup over a piece of property they jointly owned. How Connor had sold it, forging his son's name and keeping the proceeds. How the son had moved his own family away and forbidden any of them ever to have contact with the senior Connors.

The story sounded distinctly secondhand and well rehearsed to Howard. Was any of it true? In his experience even the most accomplished liars or gossips included at least one element of the truth. Sometimes in spite of not meaning to do so.

He'd call Chief Simpson later and ask if he'd heard this story. The Connors lived in Simpson's patch. He'd know. Before Walker left the two old ladies, he asked if they could make him a list of all their friends who'd visited here while Mr. Connor was a patient.

He frankly didn't think this was going to be of any help, but it was his duty to gather as much information as he could find out and sift through it repeatedly. In two previous cases, one of the most trivial facts he'd gleaned had turned out to be the key to solving the crime. His first superior had told him that at least ninety percent of what the police discovered wasn't useful, but to keep everything written down, so as not to lose the ten percent that counted.

When he finally got away from Miss Smith and Miss Jones, the Harbinger boys had just come into the living room. Harry was telling Miss Twibell that all their duplicate measurements so far had matched the first ones and they had their list of what they needed from Poughkeepsie.

Would she be able to advance them that part of the payment so they could purchase it?

Miss Twibell went to get her checkbook. The account was in a Poughkeepsie bank and they wouldn't have trouble cashing it. Unless it was one of the banks that couldn't operate now. What would she do if that was true? She didn't have that much cash on hand.

When she'd left, Harry turned around to take the last measurement of the storeroom and stopped in his tracks. "Where did all the stuff on the wall go?"

"Everybody pitched in and put it in another room," Walker said. "Robert and I took down the glass cabinet doors and the main door. We would have taken down the counter and empty cabinets if we'd known how to."

"Thanks for taking care of this. It was the part of the job we were dreading," Harry admitted. "Since the two of you are still here, could you help us take down the upper cabinet? It's too heavy for just two of us to manage."

Walker and Robert served as "holder-uppers" while Harry and his brother pulled the nails out. When the cabinet started to wobble, Harry said, "Pull the bottom out slightly so it doesn't fall on you."

Suddenly the last two nails near the top came out and both Robert and Howard groaned at the shock of how heavy the cabinet was, even empty and with the glass doors removed. After the four of them carried it out into the hall, Robert said, "I have to take the laundry down."

Howard said, "And I have to go back to my office to make some telephone calls and make notes."

Lily, who'd stayed to observe, whispered to Betty, "Those are just excuses. Both of them are red in the face and gasping."

They smiled at each other smugly.

CHAPTER TWELVE

Chief Walker helped Robert haul the big laundry bin down to the first floor. "Aren't you going to help me take it down to the basement?" Robert asked.

"You don't need me. You just put yourself in this position to escape helping with that heavy counter."

"So did you."

"No, I really do need to make a phone call from my office," Howard said. As he went out the front door and closed it behind him, he turned back and tested whether it had locked behind him, and was pleased with the result. Maybe the staff wasn't as sloppy about their safety and that of their patients as he had feared.

As he went toward the police car, he spotted Mr. Far-leigh coming around the corner of the house pushing a wheelbarrow. Howard would have liked to talk to him but knew it would frighten the man. So he just smiled and waved. Farleigh nodded and continued wherever he was headed.

Howard realized he'd noticed cooking smells on the first floor wafting up from the kitchen below and was now suddenly hungry. The woman who ran the boardinghouse always served lumpy, sticky porridge with burnt toast on Friday mornings. He'd learned to avoid eating breakfast on Fridays.

He stopped by Mabel's cafe and asked for a sandwich to take to work. As he waited, one of the Communists who thought no one knew they met in Mabel's back room, came out the door, pirouetted around awkwardly, and went back in. Howard was hard-pressed not to laugh. He knew the man was warning the others that the Law was standing at the counter.

He'd been alarmed when he learned of them. But he soon discovered through the town grapevine that they were virtually harmless. Most of them were middle-aged farmers who talked mostly about crops instead of political theories. In fact, it was said that they were still arguing from time to time about who would be the leader of the cell.

He took his sandwich to his office in the jail and ate it with a glass of cold water and a few stale crackers he found in a desk drawer. Then he called Chief Simpson in Beacon. There were three operators at the Voorburg telephone exchange. Two always listened in. One didn't. He'd learned to recognize their voices, and now said, "This will be a private call. Don't listen."

In an offended voice, the operator said, "I'll connect you."

Ed Simpson answered the phone. He must have been sitting right next to it. "Nice to hear from you, Chief Walker."

Walker said, "I'm calling to ask what you know about the Connor family."

"Sean and his wife have been feuding with each other and most of their neighbors for years. Not a happy family."

He went on to explain what they'd done to each other, and it matched fairly well with what Miss Smith had said. There had been a forgery of a deed. Stefan, the only son of Mr. and Mrs. Connor, had broken off all communication with his parents. The son had two sons of his own. Apparently Mr. and Mrs. Connor had always been at daggers drawn with each other. Aidan, the older of their two grandsons, had gone to New York City to do some sort of construction work a couple months ago on one of those big buildings that were going up everywhere in the city.

"What about the younger son?" Walker asked.

"Word leaks back that he's got some sort of bus and goes from town to town selling drugstore stuff like shaving cream. Of course, in light of the family feud, he's never visited his grandparents as far as anyone knows."

"Thanks, Ed. This corroborates what I've heard from a gossiping lady I wasn't sure I could trust. You haven't happened to hear where the second grandson is now?"

"I'm sorry. I have no idea. You could call the city halls in smaller towns hereabout."

"I'd thought of that, but my budget doesn't allow that many calls. Thanks again."

A little after lunchtime, Mrs. Connor paid an unexpected visit to the nursing home, railing at Miss Twibell for holding up Mr. Connor's funeral.

"You sent him to that funeral home," she said angrily. "Now they won't let me bury him."

Miss Twibell wasn't of a mind to be especially pleasant today to a woman berating her without cause. She had other things on her mind.

The progress of the dumbwaiter was one of those things. She was waiting anxiously for the Harbinger boys to get back with the necessary tools and hardware to install it. And she was fretting, about whether the bank would be open so they could cash her check. She knew the Harbingers had said they couldn't start until Sunday, but she held out hope they'd come back later that afternoon. She wanted the dumbwaiter, but hated the disruption its installation was causing. Nobody could find anything.

Moreover, she had to constantly herd Mattie back to bed. The girl kept disappearing, claiming she'd just slipped into the bathroom for a bit, or wanted to see what Mr. Farleigh was doing outside.

Miss Twibell didn't bother to explain her abruptness. "Mrs. Connor, there is simply nothing I can do about the body being held. You need to sort this out with your attorney."

"He's not 'my' attorney," Mrs. Connor snapped. "He's my husband's. And what's more, he's not in town. He and his wife have gone to California to be there for the birth of their first grandchild."

"Why can't his secretary phone him and let him know about your problem?"

"She's scared of running the phone bill up. And claims—I know she's lying about this—that she doesn't even know what city they're in. This is idiocy. I want him buried in my family's graveyard on our land. He's dead. He no longer has the right to make a decision. And the funeral home also claims they don't even have a valid death certificate yet."

"Are you sure they said that?" Miss Twibell asked.

"Their exact words."

"This *is* something I can fix. Sit down and I'll contact Dr. Polhemus."

"I'll come with you. I want a word or two with him."

Miss Twibell said firmly, "No. You will not. Sit down

here and wait." She hadn't been sworn to secrecy but didn't want Mrs. Connor eavesdropping if she had to explain what the judge had said in the hearing. Miss Twibell didn't know if anyone had yet told Mrs. Connor that her husband had been smothered to death. She didn't wish to be the one to reveal this and set off more fireworks.

Lily came into the room as this conversation was ending and said, "Oh, Mrs. Connor, I haven't had the chance to say how sorry I was about your husband's passing away. I'll call down to the kitchen to get you a cup of coffee. Or would you prefer tea?"

While this foolish but helpful talk was going on, Miss Twibell slipped silently out the door and went to her suite, locking Mrs. Connor out.

Miss Twibell was back in a few minutes to find Mrs. Connor doing her whole rant again for Lily's and Betty's enlightenment. Both of them pretended to sympathize with her plight. Mrs. Connor obviously thrived on this concern for her from nice young ladies.

Miss Twibell smiled gratefully at the two young women and said to Mrs. Connor, "It's taken care of. In a way. Of course the actual death certificate hasn't been officially approved by the state yet, but Dr. Polhemus is calling the funeral home and telling them what it says and they will probably release Mr. Connor for burial by tomorrow."

Mrs. Connor said, "Very well. I'll check with the funeral home later today instead of wasting my time driving back here tomorrow." And with that, she departed just as the cook's skivvy arrived with coffee, cups and saucers, and a plate of cookies.

The skivvy said, "I'll take this back since your guest has left."

"You'll do no such thing," Miss Twibell said. "We need it ourselves." When the skivvy was gone, Miss Twibell looked at Lily and Betty and added, "I didn't hear anything that sounded like 'thank you' from Mrs. Connor. Betty, you pour. And give me a little extra sugar, please."

When the three of them had consumed this treat to the last drop and crumb, Miss Twibell went to check on Mattie.

"Where has she gone this time?" she asked Lily and Betty.

"I checked her an hour ago," Betty said. "When I left she was reading a book."

Miss Twibell looked for Mattie in the bathroom. Then came back and ducked into the storeroom. Her next effort was to knock on Miss Smith's and Miss Jones's door.

"Come in," Miss Smith chirped.

Mattie was sitting on the edge of Miss Smith's bed, her hands full of yarn, taking a knitting lesson.

Miss Twibell said, "Mattie, I'd like to have a word with you in your own room."

Mattie followed, casting a sad look at Betty and Lily as she passed them.

"Mattie," Miss Twibell said after closing the door,

"you've always been good at taking my orders. You've never failed to do what I ask of you promptly and efficiently."

"Thank you, ma'am," Mattie said, looking down at the floor.

"Look at me when I'm speaking to you, dear. You're a good nurse. But you're not a nurse now. You're a patient. You must still do as I tell you. You're going to stop wandering around without my permission. If you fail, you may find yourself without a job here when you're well."

Mattie started sniffling and Miss Twibell pushed a clean handkerchief into her hand.

"Don't make a scene," Miss Twibell said. "Here are the rules. Your breakfast will be brought to your room. If your breathing, blood pressure, and heartbeat are satisfactory or better, you may, with my permission, come out and sit in the living room from ten to eleven. And after lunch in your own room, under the same conditions, you may also come out from three to four in the afternoon after your nap. If you need anything, just push the bell next to your bed."

Mattie wiped her nose, sniffed one last time, and said, "I'm sorry I've been naughty. It's just so boring staying in bed all day."

"I know it is, dear. But the last two times I've checked you, you've made no improvement. That's why you must obey the rules. I couldn't face your mother and father if you became more ill under my care. I want to hear your promise."

"I promise," Mattie said, completely cowed by this conversation.

Miss Twibell came out of Mattie's room, closed the door, and told Lily and Betty the rules she'd given Mattie. "You two must keep a close eye on her as well. I will not tolerate patients who are not getting better taking off on their own."

"Miss Twibell," Betty said, "I agree with you. But Mattie's used to being a hard worker and she must be lonely and frustrated."

"I know that. It doesn't mean she can't have a little company. Maybe each of you could play cards with her or read to her or just drop in for a chat once in a while to keep her spirits up. That's part of the healing process. Take Mr. Brewster along from time to time. He's so cheerful. But it isn't appropriate for him to be in her room alone."

"We'll do that," Lily said. "Are your feet getting better?"

"Much better today. Thank you for asking. Now I must go back to my rooms and work on the bill paying. Let me know immediately if the Harbinger boys come back with their materials this afternoon."

When Miss Twibell was gone, Betty said, "I've never known her to be this cranky."

"It's her feet hurting," Lily said. "Having to deal with Mrs. Connor, and dealing with the mess the dumbwaiter project is making, I imagine. We can't blame her. I'd be cranky, too, if I were in her shoes—or carpet slippers."

CHAPTER THIRTEEN

Saturday, March 11

Early Saturday, Chief of Police Simpson called Howard back. "I hate to say this, seeing as how I know you're working on the Connor case . . ."

"How do you know Connor's death is a case?"

"I just assumed it was. I kept expecting for years that someone would bump him off someday. When you called yesterday asking about the Connor family problems, it seemed to me to confirm it. Am I wrong?"

"No, you're not. But what do you need?"

"Help from you. I have an unidentified body here. It's in pretty bad shape. But then so am I. Gout again in both big toes. And my deputy has only been on the job one week. So far he seems a darn timid type. I can't trust him to question the neighbors who were close to the scene of the crime. He's not up to asking rude questions yet, and I can hardly walk across the room, much less all over town."

"I'm sorry. I have my own case to work on. I'm not getting anywhere with it. I'm going to have question a lot more people."

"Just one day. Say tomorrow. You might get some information up here about your case while you're helping with mine."

Howard thought for a moment. All he could do about the death of Sean Connor was question everyone at the nursing home—probably over and over. Everybody who lived or worked at Miss Twibell's nursing home. Everyone who had visited during those three months that Connor stayed. He didn't have all his questions lined up yet. "Okay. Half a day only. Where should we meet?"

"Why don't you come over to my house," Chief Simpson said, and gave him directions. "I'll be in your debt anytime you need me."

"You can count on me to take you up on that someday."

Walker called the telephone exchange early on Sunday and told the girl on duty that if she needed him, to ring Chief Simpson in Beacon. Then he put gas in the police car and headed out.

Mrs. Simpson came to the door. "Come in, Chief Walker. Ed's in the parlor. I have coffee and muffins set out. Just have Ed bellow if either of you needs more. I'll be in the kitchen."

Howard had seen Simpson only twice before and that was two years earlier. Now he thought, no wonder the man suffered from gout—he had put on at least thirty pounds since then. Was it a drinking problem, or had he been eating too much rich food for the whole two years?

They chatted for few minutes about the last time they'd had occasion to meet. Howard ate one muffin and drank a little of his coffee. Simpson had three muffins and finished his coffee. Mrs. Simpson had left the carafe on a side table, and Howard poured the man another cup.

"So fill me in so I can get started. Where was the body found? And when?" Walker asked.

"Up in the hills above. There's a small but deep lake. I'd guess some of the neighbors have lost cows in it over the years. It's not fit for swimming. It's scummy. But the young people around here sometimes crawl down the sides of the slope and ice-skate there. When the ice broke up last week, the body of a young man, quite bloated, came to the surface. Must have gone in there in the winter.

"The first odd thing my former deputy officer noticed," he went on, "was that the body had one ice skate on, and the other foot had been gnawed on, probably under water. We thought at first he might have been sitting on the steep bank putting on the first skate when some animal attacked him."

Walker thought it was time to get to the point. "And later?" he urged.

"Later we found that the upper front part of his skull was crushed, and then when he was turned over, that there was buckshot in his shoulders and upper back. Someone shot him, and the impact must have thrust him headfirst, and he broke the ice thoroughly enough for him to sink and drift under it."

"So it's clearly murder? Or an attack by somebody that resulted in his death? Can anyone determine when the ice was at a point that a hole large enough would have formed? Was this man extra heavy? Or thin?"

Simpson thought for a few minutes. "There was the bloating to account for, but the autopsy showed that it was a young man, possibly twenty years old or a little younger, and small-boned. About five feet six. But he could have been fat to start with. As for the condition of the ice, it never crossed my mind. That's one of the things you'll have to ask the neighbors about. Sometimes it gets damned cold early in those secluded little valleys up there. But the locals say it's good fishing. I don't fish, so I can't swear to that."

"What about clothing and hair color?"

"Hard to tell. What little hair was left was light brown with a hint of red. The red could be a result of the horrible quality of the water though. There wasn't much of his clothing left except the one ice skate. The fish and snails and whatnot must have fed on him. You'd of thought the cold would preserve a body. On the other hand, in the winter, fish don't feed on bugs and such that fall in over the other three seasons. Maybe there's something nasty in the water that dissolves clothing."

At that point Simpson's deputy arrived, and Mrs. Simpson set out another plate of muffins and a cup of coffee for him.

"This is Deputy Ron Parker," Chief Simpson said. Howard thought he could actually see the boy blush slightly. He seemed very shy. He also looked too young to know anything about police work. No wonder Chief Simpson needed help. Howard just wished he'd asked someone else for it.

"Did the pathologist suggest how long the boy had been in the water?" Walker asked.

"He says that it was probably all winter, and I had reason to believe he went in sometime around Christmas. You see, there's a dotty old woman who lives in a shack close to the lake. She called a few days after the holiday with a bizarre story about a man banging on her door and telling her to call the police because he'd seen someone shoot a person who fell into the lake, breaking through the ice and disappearing."

"You investigated this?"

"Reluctantly. By the time she got around to calling, there was a hard freeze and significant snow cover. There wasn't any way to guess if this was even true, or where to try to brush away the snow and cut through the ice," Simpson explained.

"I suppose we should start investigating," Walker said.

Deputy Parker, who'd eaten half his muffin, dropped

it back on his plate as if it had suddenly become too hot to eat.

He almost ran out of the house, car keys jangling, and opened the passenger door of the police car for his superior with a small nod that was almost a bow. He drove slowly and carefully toward the hills, as if he were still learning the fine points of how a clutch worked.

Howard, in a brief moment of pity, asked, "Would you prefer that I drive? And you give directions?"

"Oh, yes please, sir," Parker said as if addressing a kindly god. "I know how to drive a tractor, but I don't yet understand this automobile."

They changed seats and Parker directed Chief Walker to the only long view of the lake where the body had been found. When Walker saw it, he understood how it could have happened. The hills around it were steep. It wasn't a lake that water flowed into and then out of. It looked more like a sinkhole that a long, skinny mass of underlying sand had washed out from under, making the stone above collapse.

There was one small flat area near the shore, with a slight rise at the left side that was muddy. It half concealed some sort of old structure. The boy must have put on one skate, planning to put on the other, leave his shoes behind, and scoot down from the rise.

"Did the former deputy find the other skate or his shoes?" Walker asked.

"No, sir."

"Did anyone examine the trees for buckshot to guess how far away the shooter was?"

"I don't think so, sir."

"Then it needs to be done. But I don't have the time. Your chief is going to have to find someone else to do that. Let's get in the car and look for witnesses. We passed two driveways on the way up here."

Poor Deputy Parker started to give himself a slap on the head but managed to abort the gesture and clap his hand to his side. "That's a good idea, sir."

At the first farm they came to, the ground rose slightly between the barn and the lake, then dropped steeply. As the two uniformed officers faced the lake, a voice called, "Hoy! Whatta you doin'? Get back from the edge."

Chief Walker turned and walked toward the man, hand held out to shake the farmer's. "I'm Chief of Police Walker from Voorburg, giving Chief Simpson and Deputy Parker here a little help."

"Yeah. I hear Ed's laid up with the gout. I'm Dan Kincade. Been farmin' here for ten years going on eleven."

"Was it you who spotted the body?"

"Nope, it was my kid Jimmy, and I whopped him hard fer getting near to the edge. I've told him it's crumbling. I don't even go to the edge. For one thing, that lake stinks like hell in the summer. When the wind picks it up jest

right, you can smell it clear up here. Makes me retch. Figured anyway Jimmy was mistaking a dead cow for a person. Over the years, that's happened a couple times. Some
dumb cow or sheep gets outta its fence and falls in. Wasn't
until a couple days later I heard it was a person."

"Someone told me it's good fishing though," Howard
said.

"Only for those what have no sense of smell, I reckon.
How anybody could eat a fish that grew in that muck must
have no sense of smell or taste."

"Do you have any idea of who the dead man was?"

"No idea a'tall. Sorry to say."

"Thank you for your time," Howard said, shaking Kincade's hand again, and headed back to the automobile.

As they located the other driveway he'd seen on the way
up the hill, he stopped before turning in. "Did you watch
and listen, Parker?"

"Yes, sir."

"Then you do this one."

"Oh, I don't think I could, sir."

"But you will," Howard said. "This doesn't look like a
farm. Just a nice house. We'll go to the front door."

Deputy Parker waited for Chief Walker to knock. And
waited. And waited. Then he realized it was his job.
Parker's knuckles barely brushed the door.

"Harder," Walker advised.

This time Deputy Parker knocked so hard he hurt his hand.

In a moment a young woman with curly fair hair, a big toothy smile, and a baby on her hip opened the door. "Boy oh boy, was that *some* knock. How can I help you?"

"We have some questions to ask you about the body found in the lake behind your house," Parker said in a firmer voice than Howard had expected.

"Then come around the side of the house."

They found themselves in a small backyard with a high, obviously new, stone wall across the back and up both sides. There were certainly signs of spring here. A forsythia bush was loaded with buds. So was a plum tree. Fresh new blades of irises were already up, but no buds showed yet.

"You like this?" the young woman asked. "I'm proud of it. I never had experience with gardening until we moved here three years ago. It's ahead of most gardens hereabout because it's enclosed from the winds and the stone wall holds the heat of the sun."

"That's why you built it?" Howard asked.

"Oh, no. It was to divert the awful smell from that nasty little lake below."

Parker took over again, which pleased Walker. "Ma'am, you probably can't see over it. Only a very tall person might."

She smiled. "So far none of our guests have wanted to

even try. I suppose with a ladder you could see the lake. And maybe even smell it."

"Before you had the wall, could you see the lake?" Parker asked.

"Barely. It's heavily wooded between here and there."

"So you never saw anyone skating in the winter or fishing in the summer?"

"No, we didn't. But we weren't interested in looking at it, much less having to smell it."

Parker smiled and her and said, "Thank you very much for your time. And that's such a pretty baby you have."

As the woman went back inside by the back door and they walked along the side yard, Howard stopped and said, "You did that very well, Parker. You started out polite, and not threatening. You asked good questions. You ended the conversation right. You're on the right track, young man."

"Oh—thank you, sir. Thank you so much."

For fear that Deputy Parker would go overboard and cry or try to shake his hand, Walker quickly walked around the car and started the engine. They hadn't found out anything of use. But he'd given Parker some confidence, returning the favor his first superior officer had bestowed on him so many years ago.

CHAPTER FOURTEEN

As Chief Walker and Deputy Parker drove around hunting another house that might overlook the lake, Walker pulled over at a wide place in the road.

"Deputy Parker, I have a feeling that Chief Simpson wasn't comfortable telling me as much as he knew about this body being found. I don't want to suggest that you tell tales out of school, but I must. Do you know why he was so vague?"

"I wouldn't have known anything more than what he said to you, except that I ran into another deputy I went to school with, who was at the dotty old woman's house twice. I met him a day after I got this job."

"So who found the body when it floated up recently? Kincade's son saw it but wasn't believed. Someone must have spotted it from close enough to see that it was human."

"It was the same old woman, sir. She fishes there in the summer. She's closer to the lake than anyone else."

"She lives close to that smell and it was the first time she noticed?"

"She really is dotty, sir, my school friend said. Maybe it's the stink that made her that way. Her story last winter was that she was watching a peculiar-looking hiker climbing around on a hill above her house. She kept her binoculars on him. He suddenly started running toward her, falling down several times and cursing loudly. Must have scared her clean out of whatever wits she still might have had. She locked her door and covered the windows before he reached her house. He banged on her door, she told Chief Simpson and his former deputy. He shouted at her to call the police because there was a body in the lake."

"Does a woman like that have a phone? You wouldn't think anyone would run a phone line down there."

"Yes, sir. She does. I heard that the men who go to fish there got together and paid for a phone line for her so they could make calls telling their wives or sweethearts when they might be home. She uses it a lot."

"So she called the police, I assume. What happened next?"

"She says she went to a window, opened it an inch or two, and shouted that she'd made the call. The police would be there soon. Nobody replied, she said. So she went from window to window, peeking out and looking for where the man had gone. She's got windows all around the house."

"Did the police spot the body when she called again a few days ago?"

"Yes, sir. They first called for help from a few other nearby towns to drag the body out. Chief Simpson told me two of them threw up before they could haul the body away. It was quite a while later that they questioned her about how she found out about the body. There was a little rise that would have obscured her view, you see. By the time they spoke to her, she'd had plenty of time to make up a story. The one I just told you, sir."

"You didn't believe it was the truth?"

"I wasn't here yet, sir. But nobody who was believed her. Before that, her last call to the police was to complain about the bear who destroyed her shed and took away the wood to make a place in the woods to live in himself."

Walker smiled. "Go on."

"It seems the bear left behind his pry bar, sir. And a frayed piece of rope." Even Deputy Parker thought this was funny. So did Howard, who chuckled.

"So how did she describe this man she'd been watching with her binoculars back in December?" Howard asked.

"He was a Commie. She could tell by the way he dressed. He carried a big old stick and had long dirty black hair, slanted eyes, and wore a red beret. He was coming to kidnap her and take her to Russia, she feared, sir."

Walker put his head close to the steering wheel and pretended to be banging his forehead on it. "That's the craziest thing I've ever heard. No, maybe the tool-laden bear story is worse."

"You can understand why nobody took notice, sir. She probably was just taking a walk to see if the ice had all melted on the lake yet and saw the body floating."

Howard pulled himself together and asked, "Has anybody interviewed her again?"

"No, sir. I never heard they did. You can ask Chief Simpson though."

Instead of going directly to Chief Simpson's home, they stopped at a local greasy spoon restaurant on Route 9. It was really too early for lunch, but Howard hadn't had breakfast. He ordered a bottle of beer and a toasted cheese sandwich with sour pickles on the side. Deputy Parker ordered a soda, and ham and bean soup with lots of crackers.

While they ate, Howard asked Parker about his life and how and why he'd joined the police.

Parker told him that he was from a small town on the other side of the river about ten miles north of Beacon. The town was so small that Howard hadn't ever heard of it.

The deputy went on to say that he'd always wanted to

be a policeman ever since he fell off his bicycle when he was eight years old, and a very nice policeman had taken him to the hospital to be checked out and driven him home and helped his dad repair the damage to the bicycle. So when he turned eighteen, his parents gave him a third of the corn profits and told him to use it to attend a police school. Parker named the school, but Walker had never heard of it either. Parker had attended for a year before the money had almost run out. But he thought he might get a job anyway and study more in his free time.

"Anyway," he continued, "I took off and went down-river to every police station I could find. Nobody needed me. I had almost no money left and slept in the woods at night in my farm clothes to keep my one suit clean. I finally crossed the river on a ferry because the owner was my mother's second cousin and he didn't charge me. I ended up in Beacon working my way back north. Chief Simpson had just lost his deputy because the deputy took off with his family to California."

They finished their lunch and went back to Chief Simpson's house. "We've struck out," Walker admitted. "We questioned two households that overlook that lake. But nobody bothers to look at it. One young couple even put up a big stone wall in an attempt to cut out the sight and smell of it."

"So where do you suggest we go from here?" Chief Simpson asked.

"I think if it were me, I'd put a notice in a lot of nearby newspapers, asking if anyone knew of a young man who'd gone missing in the middle of last winter and to contact you if they do."

"But a great many whole families have gone off to California," Ed Simpson replied.

"This isn't a whole family. It's one young man. It might not be worth it, but it could give you a couple of leads," Walker said. Glancing at his watch, he added, "I still have a little time to spare while I'm here. Have you sent anyone to the crazy old woman who reported the body that floated up? She might have remembered something accurate since that day."

"I'm sorry I forgot to tell you about her. She was obviously an unreliable witness and I'd already put her out of my mind. Did Deputy Parker tell you about the bear?"

"Yes," Howard said with a laugh. "But she might have lucid moments. "If Deputy Parker doesn't mind and can find the place, I'd like to talk to her. It's the last thing I can think of doing."

Deputy Parker reluctantly agreed, but suggested they wear scarves or something to avoid the smell.

"Good idea, except that would probably scare her right around the bend. She'd think we were bandits."

They set out, got lost a few times, and finally found a steep unmown track that led down to the lake. They had to abandon the police car two-thirds of the way and walk the rest. "Do you know this woman's name?" Walker asked Parker.

"No, sir. I don't think anyone told me what it was."

When they reached the house, if you could imagine anyone living in it calling it a home, Walker almost turned around. It was a dreadful place and the smell of the lake up close was horrendous. But they'd come this far and might as well follow up.

He knocked at the door and said loudly, "We're the police and we need some advice from you, ma'am."

The door opened a crack and a pale blue eye peered at them. Apparently she approved of them as they were both in police uniforms, and pulled the door wider and invited them in. Three scruffy cats and one skinny kitten ran past them outside. There seemed to be dozens of other cats inside. Two were sleeping in a filthy sink, and there was a whole row of them above the small fireplace.

It was a log house and must have been at least eighty years old. The original chinking had long since disappeared, and the cracks were now stuffed with bits of old newspapers. The woman herself was small and wrapped in what looked like an assortment of rags strung together. He suspected she wasn't nearly as old as she looked and had just lived a very hard life.

"I've never had police officers here," she said, indicating that they should sit down on two of the three chairs at a table in the middle of the room. Cats occupied them right now but she started scattering them.

"No, thank you, ma'am. We'll stand," Deputy Parker said firmly.

"I've heard that you *have* had police officers here before," Walker said.

She tilted her head, almost flirtatiously. "Now, who would say that about me?"

"I don't remember," Walker said. "What we need to know is your description of the man who saw the body go into the lake last December."

She made a noise that must have been meant as a laugh but sounded more like a chicken being strangled. "What man? What body? I don't know what you're talking about."

Howard made a quick half-bow and headed for the door. Parker followed close behind him, saying, "Thank you for your help. Good day to you, ma'am."

As they got far enough back up the hill to speak without gagging at the smell of the lake, Howard said, "I don't think this was her lucid day. If, in fact, she ever has one. I've wasted your time and mine."

"Still, sir, it *was* interesting. How could anyone live in a place like that? What does she feed all those cats?"

When Howard arrived back in Voorburg and showered to get the smell of the lake out, he rang up Chief Simpson's home and said to him, "Keep Deputy Parker. He's going to turn out well if you give him a chance."

"You really think so?" There was serious doubt in his voice.

"I know so. If you ever find a replacement for him, send Parker to me."

CHAPTER FIFTEEN

On Sunday morning, while Howard was roaming around with Deputy Parker, the Harbinger boys returned to Miss Twibell's nursing home. They brought the necessary tools up to the second floor, cut a new spot at the far left end of the storeroom wall and installed the old door, cutting through the floor to the small bathroom below. Then they headed out with their tools to cut through the first floor to the basement.

"Hold on," Miss Twibell said. "What are you doing? Why are you taking the tools away?"

"To work on the next step. The bathroom floor to the basement," Harry replied.

"And leave everything—all the equipment we need every day to take care of our patients—all over that extra room?" she asked.

"But it's more practical to get the way cleared all the way down to the basement," Harry explained.

"Practical for you, perhaps. Not practical for me. I'm sorry, but I'm going to have to insist that you clean up the storeroom, put the upper and lower cabinets in their new places, and install the counter. Robert can probably remember how to put the glass doors back on, since he helped to take them off."

The argument went on for quite a while. Concerns over efficiency, timing, cleaning up, and testing the system were discussed at some length, and with considerable heat.

In the end, Miss Twibell prevailed, which she knew how to do better than the young men did. By the end of the day, the work was done the way she wanted it. They gave the room and the door a fresh coat of paint, shoved the debris down the hole, and even put up sturdy hooks in pairs so that mops, brushes, and dustpans could be hung upside down on the walls instead of leaning against them higgledy-piggledy, and tripping up people working in the room.

There were also places to hang the buckets for washing and rinsing the floors, and a small cabinet in which to store gloves and clean rags was installed in the corner. Then they put the old cabinets and counter and cabinet doors into the new arrangement. They even mopped the floor of the workroom and temporarily nailed down two planks so that nobody could possibly fall through the hole.

For this extra work, against their theoretical better judgment, Harry and Jim were rewarded with double portions of lunch and a nice cash tip, with Miss Twibell's most gracious thanks.

At that, there was a general exhalation of the held breaths that had prevailed among the staff all morning.

But as soon as the young men had finished their lunch, burped contentedly, and taken away their tools, Miss Twibell went into high gear again, to everyone's sorrow.

"Betty, Mr. and Miss Brewster, I'll need your help now. We'll start with things that go in the storeroom. You can bring in the large things first. And while you're putting them away, I'll go through the smaller items that go in the outside cabinets. It's time to purge some things that are past their prime and replace them. I'll make a list as I go."

Chief Howard Walker, on the other hand, completely wasted what he'd hoped would be a productive Sunday afternoon that he'd hoped to use clearing up his office and filing masses of piled-up paperwork.

Instead, he interviewed most of the women on Miss Smith's list of addresses for the knitting circle. He managed to interrupt several Sunday after-church dinners, chatting with housewives who came to the door in their special Sunday aprons. Most of them showed alarm when he showed up. Some also showed impatience at the interruption when they realized he hadn't shown up for any important reason, such as complaints against their children for missing school or breaking someone's window.

None of them had anything of consequence to say about Mr. Connor, alive or dead, except the few that complained that early on, when he still had his strength, he'd been rude when they met in the living room at the nursing home—making loud, nasty remarks about the noise of cackling hens with nothing worthwhile to do except gossip and laugh.

Howard went back to his office in the boardinghouse, which reeked of cabbage even more than it normally did, and furiously filed paperwork, throwing a good quarter of it out as useless to keep any longer.

Then he went over all the notes he'd made on the death of Sean Connor. He often found that taking copious notes was helpful. Most often, if he took down enough details, some of the items would fall together and mean more than he originally thought they did. No luck today, though. He, like everyone else, couldn't come up with a viable theory as to why anyone would have a motive to kill someone who was about to die within a matter of hours anyway.

He kept coming back to his notes about Mark Farleigh though. He didn't really know anything about this man except what Miss Twibell had told him. He had no reason to think she'd lie about him. But maybe her own perception of Farleigh wasn't true. How could he possibly question a man who would only speak to one person, and then merely with a word or two of acknowledgment?

It was clear that Farleigh was a deeply disturbed individual. So were many of the men who had served in the Great War. The only ones who seemed to be able to put it out of their minds were the most stupid and insensitive of them. Simply thinking about what they'd had to endure filled him with horror. More than one soldier, just in Voorburg alone, had committed suicide because they couldn't get their minds off the constant fear, the smell of the mustard gas, the mutilations they'd suffered, or those they themselves had inflicted on strangers.

Howard found himself wondering if Sean Connor had been a soldier in that war as well. Could there be some obscure motive there? Could Farleigh have met him on a battlefield? He made a note to find out whether Connor had enlisted.

Then he turned his thoughts to the nursing assistant, Betty. She had borne the brunt of Sean Connor's bone-deep nastiness. Having to clean and dress his knee regularly must have put a strain on both him and her. Connor undoubtedly would have been rude to her. Perhaps even violent. Maybe she had simply reached a breaking point and could no longer stand to be anywhere near him.

On the other hand, she did admit, even though she needn't have, that the last time she checked on him, she merely looked in the door instead of checking his breathing or blood pressure or temperature. That bit of honesty about a failure to do her job thoroughly was in her favor.

What did he know of the Connor family, in fact? He'd heard Miss Smith's version of how Sean Connor had alienated his only son. Chief Ed Simpson had verified it. But what about the rest of his family? His wife had grown to dislike him. But what wife wouldn't if she lived with a man like that? Did he have daughters, sisters, or brothers he had also lied to or cheated? Another note was made to check further into family relations. That might be something Jack Summer would like to snoop around and find out. Jack was good at snooping.

He considered Miss Twibell out of the picture as a suspect. She had the heart of a saint and the bossiness of a general. She'd probably treated a great many other sick, cranky patients over the years. If she couldn't put up with them, she wouldn't have kept taking them in over such a long time. It would have been easier to simply take in boarders and get to choose who could live in her home, instead of having to put up with someone like Sean Connor.

Finally he closed his notebook and let his mind just wander. Sometimes that helped. This time it didn't.

Lily, Robert, and Betty were exhausted at the end of their Sunday duty. Miss Twibell had worked them hard all afternoon. None of them had even had the opportunity to sit down the whole time she had them restocking the storeroom and the pharmacy. They'd been run off their feet, criticized for putting things in the wrong places, complimented when they did it right. But they'd worked like horses hauling mops, buckets, flasks, bottles, rolls of bandages, and laundry baskets. To be fair, Lily knew that Miss Twibell, in spite of her feet still hurting, had worked as hard as they had. Miss Twibell, the tallest of the women, had even held the glass doors in place while Robert reattached them.

Robert was unusually anxious to get home. President Roosevelt was going to give his first "Fireside Chat" on the radio that evening, and he didn't want to miss it.

When they were finally released and dragged themselves back to Grace and Favor, Robert called Howard Walker. "Want to have dinner here and listen to the President with us?"

"I'd be grateful for that," Howard said. "It's been a long day. Dinner here is cabbage, and the rest of the boarders will talk through the radio show. You're sure it's okay with Mrs. Prinney?"

"She's agreed. She loves cooking, and the more she can feed, the happier she is."

Dinner was wonderful but Lily nearly fell asleep over her plate. She even turned down dessert. "I'm so tired and I smell of disinfectant and soap. I'm taking a bath and going to bed. Robert, you can tell me tomorrow what the President said."

Jack Summer had also been invited, because Robert knew that the reporter's radio didn't work as well as the one at Grace and Favor and that he'd want to listen. And he thought that maybe after the program he could pry some more information out of Chief Walker.

Mrs. Prinney and Mimi, the maid, hustled the plates to the kitchen to soak so that they could listen, too. Miss Phoebe Twinkle, one of their two boarders, helped out with this as well. Mrs. Tarkington, the other boarder and school principal, was exempted from this chore.

The men all went into the library to smoke and have some nice smooth old whiskey while Robert made sure the radio was tuned right. They put out their cigars and cigarettes and opened the French doors for a few minutes to air out the room before Mimi, Mrs. Prinney, Miss Twinkle, and Mrs. Tarkington joined them.

They all sat and stared at the radio as Franklin Roosevelt started speaking in a powerful, friendly, confident voice.

"My friends, I want to talk for a few minutes with the people of the United States about banking . . ."

CHAPTER SIXTEEN

Monday, March 13

Lily, having had a good night's sleep, was the first to arrive for breakfast. Only hot tea, coffee, cups, plates, and silverware were set out. Robert was next to arrive in the dining room. He poured each of them a cup of tea and sat down across the table from her.

"You're an early bird for a change," Lily said.

"So are you," Robert replied. "You have a mind that's good with arithmetic. What you do you know about how banks operate?"

"Not much," Lily said, getting up to find the sugar bowl. "You put your money in, and when you take it back out, they pay you a little bit of interest."

"You must know more than that. You once worked at a bank."

Lily had tried hard to forget that dismal part of her life when she and Robert were living in a fifth-floor cold-water apartment in New York City and too poor to even eat well.

"I only sorted checks into order by state."

"Okay, so you didn't learn much there. But what happened to your money while it was sitting in the bank earning a little interest?"

"I haven't the faintest idea."

"If the bank was keeping your money and paying you a little bit," Robert went on, slowly creeping up on the point he was about to make, "how did the bank pay the clerks? How did they pay for the gas or electricity or repairs? How did the owner of the bank always manage to live well?"

Lily frowned. "I never gave it a thought. Not even when we had lots of money in the old days. And all the pitiful money we've made since we came here is in Mr. Prinney's safe, not earning anything. So, how *do* banks make their money?"

"Pass that sugar over, would you?"

As he stirred in a heaping teaspoon of sugar, he went on, "If you'd listened to President Roosevelt last night, you'd know. The bank doesn't put your quarters, dimes, and dollar bills into a safe. They use that money. They loan it out to people at a greater interest than they pay you for your savings. They invest it in stocks and bonds and companies, and also get dividends in excess of what they pay you."

Lily's eyes lit up. "I should have realized that. The stock market collapsed. The mortgages couldn't be paid.

Which is why we're letting most of Uncle Horatio's farmers not pay right now. There aren't any dividends. That's why Voorburg's bank closed before we ever came here."

"It wasn't only Voorburg's bank," Robert said. "Thousands of banks all over the country lost money. Banks usually keep enough cash on hand to let a reasonable number of people take their money out. But as the economy got worse and worse, everybody took their money out. And the banks couldn't pay their own bills. That's why they had to close. That's how so many people lost their life savings."

"Is that what President Roosevelt was talking about last night?"

"Yes. And I admit I'd never understood it before either."

"So what does he propose to do about it?"

"Lots of things. More stringent banking laws about how much they have to keep in reserve, how much they can invest, and what they can invest in. And the Bureau of Engraving and Printing is producing a lot more money to be distributed through the twelve Federal Reserve Banks to help the few banks that still exist to survive, and as soon as possible reopen banks that weren't as irresponsible as some of the others. But only through something that's been set up called the Reconstruction Finance Corporation, which will be under the control of each individual state."

"Is it legal to just print more money?" Lily asked.

"It is now. Because Roosevelt says so. He even hinted that some bankers were criminally responsible for their investments, or even just stupid. They can only reopen under strict supervision, if at all."

Robert added in a self-satisfied tone, "Didn't I tell you Roosevelt would try anything that might help? He demanded the same powers a president would have in a real war to fight the financial war."

When they arrived at the nursing home, the dumbwaiter installation was going exceedingly well. The Harbinger boys were working in the bathroom below the storeroom and were almost through to the basement. There were coils of sturdy ropes and a platform on the ground floor, waiting to be installed. A large trash container of what Miss Twibell had purged from the extra hospital room was sitting by the front door, waiting to be taken away by Mr. Farleigh and burned.

"We might be here long enough to make use of that dumbwaiter," Robert said. "I can't wait to try it out."

Lily started the morning by mopping the pharmacy floor, while Betty brought Mattie out to sit on the sofa while her bedding was being changed. A little pot of bright green foliage with yellow flowers was sitting on the big table in front of the sofa. Mr. Farleigh must have grown it in the small glass house adjoining his workshop.

Robert was taking down the laundry when the peace and quiet was suddenly broken by Mrs. Connor coming up the stairs and shouting for Miss Twibell.

Miss Twibell emerged from her suite. "What are you doing here, Mrs. Connor?" she asked in a fairly reasonable voice.

"How could you and that nurse Betty have done this to me?" Mrs. Connor shouted.

"I have no idea what you're talking about. Come sit down in the living room and explain."

"The lawyer finally came back to Beacon," Mrs. Connor said. "He showed me the will, and you and that nurse had witnessed it. How could you have betrayed me that way?"

"Will?" Miss Twibell asked. "We did indeed witness your husband's signature on some sort of document several weeks ago. But we weren't privy to what the document was. We only signed on the last page, affirming that we'd seen him sign it in our presence. I assumed it was a deed or some other kind of document."

"It was his will," Mrs. Connor said. "He left me the house, but left the entire farm and outbuildings to our grandsons." She started sobbing bitterly. "Our grandsons! Who have grown up hating both of us!"

"How could he do that?" Miss Twibell asked. "Didn't you inherit the property from your family? Why would he be allowed to dispose of it in his will?"

Mrs. Connor finally lowered her voice. "It was my fault. I was so glad to be married instead of facing a lifetime as a lonely spinster that I imagined I could love him, and he'd love me in return because I had money, a house, and a farm." She was sobbing so hard that it was difficult to understand what she was saying. "As a sign of my gratitude, I stupidly signed off the farm to him."

"Oh, no!" Miss Twibell exclaimed. "How could you have thought that was a good idea? Did Mr. Connor suggest it?"

"No. Well, maybe he hinted at it once or twice. It was the day our son, Stefan, was born and I was so happy that I would have done anything to thank Sean for marrying me and allowing me to become a mother. I assumed, of course, that this darling baby boy would inherit the farm in his turn and take good care of us when we were old and infirm."

She put her head in her hands and sobbed, "How could I have known what a nasty man my husband would become? And how much our son and grandsons would come to hate us?"

Miss Twibell looked stricken. She patted Mrs. Connor's shoulder and glanced at Lily and Betty, who were standing and gawking helplessly. Nobody had even noticed that Mattie had silently disappeared back into her own room.

Miss Twibell finally said, "I think you should talk to the lawyer again or, better yet, hire a lawyer of your own. Explain this to him. Tell him how you signed over the farm while you were so emotional you weren't in your right mind. Maybe the provision in the will could be overturned. I assume it wasn't written until that lawyer came here. Was there a previous will leaving the farm to you or your son?"

"I don't know," Mrs. Connor croaked.

"You really need your own lawyer. Is there another one in Beacon you could hire?"

"I think so," Mrs. Connor said, and finally stopped crying. She pulled a large handkerchief out of her handbag and mopped her face. "You may be right. I can't bear the thought of our grandsons owning my farm. Neither of them knows how to run a farm. Neither of them has even spoken to me for years. This isn't right."

She rose and straightened her spine, assuming all the haughtiness she'd had before, and walked out without a word of thanks.

"Maybe I shouldn't have suggested anything," Miss Twibell said to Lily and Betty. "For a moment there, when she was letting down her hair, I had a moment of sympathy for her."

"She's reaped what she sowed," Betty said coldly.

Lily, a little more sensible and worldly than Betty, said, "Miss Twibell, I'd suggest that since Mrs. Connor made no secret of this, you tell Chief Walker what she told us."

"Why would it interest him?"

"Because he's investigating a murder."

CHAPTER SEVENTEEN

Chief Walker had spent his whole morning trying to determine whether Sean Connor had fought in the Great War. He'd finally found a military record. Connor had been a private, serving only the final year, at a desk in Newark, New Jersey. It would have been easier to simply ask Mrs. Connor. But much more unpleasant.

Still, could there be a connection between Mark Farleigh and Sean Connor? Could Farleigh have disembarked in Newark and been processed by Connor? Not likely, Walker assumed. Privates probably weren't involved in that type of work.

Could Farleigh have known him before the war? Since Farleigh was studying botany, would that have involved working on a farm? Farmers raised crops. That might be a connection. How could he find out? Ask Mrs. Connor? She'd be unlikely to remember who might have worked briefly for them after so many years had passed.

Jack Summer was getting into the habit of dropping in at the police station to catch up with what Howard had found out.

Howard told him about his Sunday morning venture to Beacon, and when he came to the bear story, Jack almost fell out of his chair laughing.

When he finally recovered, he asked, "Did you find out anything about the Connor family while you were there?"

"Not a thing. I was just helping out a friend. It was his case, not mine."

It came as something of a relief to be called to the nursing home to hear what Mrs. Connor had told Miss Twibell. It must have been something Miss Twibell didn't want the snoopy telephone girls to know. This time he didn't allow Jack to come along.

"I felt sorry for that woman until she was gone," Miss Twibell said. "Now I'm not at all sure she was telling the truth about any of it."

"Tell me, to the best of your recall, what she said," Walker requested.

Miss Twibell did so.

"She turned the farm she inherited over to her husband because she was so happy to have had a baby?" Walker said with astonishment. "The few women I've known who had a first baby wanted most for someone to take it away so they could get a little sleep."

Miss Twibell smiled. "That's often the case. And sometimes they really resent their husbands for putting them through it."

"Is that the part you didn't believe?"

"Not especially. The whole of what she said was highly emotional, and I sort of fell for it. But when she had left, I was sorry I'd advised her to get a lawyer to fight the provision in the will. Something about what she'd said suddenly seemed phony. It wasn't one thing. It was the whole story. From what I've heard about the family—and it's all pure gossip—neither of the grandchildren liked either of their grandparents. And the feeling was mutual."

"But didn't the younger boy, the one with the truck, visit his grandfather and leave samples of his wares?"

"Yes, that's true. But never when his grandmother might be around. And Mr. Connor didn't seem to give a fig for the boy or his samples. He'd tell me to throw them away or give them to someone else when the boy left."

"Are you sure it was his will that you and Betty witnessed?" Walker asked.

"Not at all. The lawyer had covered up the document and said all we had to do was watch him sign whatever it was, saying we'd seen him sign it."

"So it could have been a deed or a power of attorney or some other kind of document?"

"It could have been anything."

"Was he, in your view, competent to sign anything at that time?"

"Yes, I believe so. He wasn't all that ill when he first came here. The infection started deep in the knee only a month ago. And even then, he wasn't failing mentally, just physically."

"But he was always mean?"

"Mean, yes. But not stupid or incompetent—except socially. And he may have been mean and rude for many years before his injury, for all I know. I'd only seen him once before he came here, and that was when I was a child attending their wedding with my parents."

"Mrs. Connor didn't consider this conversation she had with you confidential, did she?"

"Absolutely not. I wouldn't have been surprised if she didn't write it up and try to get her story in the Beacon newspaper."

"Then I'll go speak with her," Walker said.

"Chief Walker, this is probably a silly idea but . . ."

"Nothing you could say would seem silly to me at this point."

"I'm wondering if the will might have been forged. Maybe it wasn't a will Betty and I witnessed. Maybe our signatures were collected to be copied to something else?"

"That's an interesting idea. Except that a good attorney probably wouldn't be fooled by it."

"What if the man who came here wasn't really an attorney? He didn't mention his name. And even if he had, all attorneys aren't reputable, you know."

After getting directions from Chief Simpson, Howard drove to the Connor home, which was a big farmhouse, built for a big family. There was a huge kitchen with an enormous oak table, five chairs on each side and one at each end. Without a big family to feed, what did they need this for? Feeding workers, possibly. He couldn't quite imagine Mrs. Connor cooking big meals for them; perhaps there was a full-time cook. Perhaps when the house belonged to her parents, they were the ones who fed workers.

She showed him into a Victorian parlor adorned with frilly doilies covering every surface. They had probably been white to start with, but were now a dun brown. Walker guessed they hadn't been washed for years, for fear they'd disintegrate if soap and water was applied. There was an old-fashioned bell jar covering a bowl of wax flowers that had faded to pale, brownish shades of pinks and greens. The walls were covered with faded floral wallpaper of big pink roses.

Walker started revising his idea of how old this house really was. He'd assumed Mrs. Connor's father had built it. But this room probably went back to her grandfather's time, at least. Perhaps that huge table and all the chairs had originally been used to accommodate a family with lots of children. He started wondering just how many other relatives the woman must have—probably dozens and dozens. And he might have to hunt down as many as he could find to question them as well.

That would involve hours of crawling up ladders to bring down title books, going to churches to find out the genealogy of the entire mob of cousins, second-cousins once-removed, and great-grandchildren's baptism dates. There simply wasn't time for all this unless he found, and stole, the family Bible.

Mrs. Connor watched him sullenly as he looked around the room, and wondered why he hadn't said anything yet. She hadn't been happy to let him in the house to snoop in the first place.

Walker finally realized he needed to question her. "What did you say to Miss Twibell when you visited her today?"

"Why would that be any of your business?"

"Because your husband's dead, and the circumstances are peculiar," he replied.

"I suppose it's the only way to get you to go away and leave me alone," she said. She told him the same story she'd told Miss Twibell, but not so emotionally. She was offended to be asked by an officer of the law about her private business, and said so. And oddly, her words sounded rehearsed to him. He wondered whether she knew yet that

her husband hadn't died of his illness but had been murdered. It was the first time he'd wondered why she wasn't
one of the witnesses when the meeting was held with the
judge. He had to ask this unpleasant question about her
impression of the reason for Mr. Connor's death.

It finally roused her to outright anger. "Of course I've
been told that he was smothered to death. But I don't
believe it, and I certainly didn't kill him, if that's your
next question. I needed him back to run the farm. He was
firm and often rude to our workers, but fair. They simply
won't take orders from me. I've already lost two of them
and the third one is suggesting it's too much work for him
to do alone. I desperately wanted Sean to get well and
come back to sort this out before planting time for this
year's crops. You'd understand this if you knew anything
about farming."

"I do know a little," he said. It was too bad that he
couldn't arrest her just because he didn't like her. He'd
never taken to belligerent women, especially those who
were taller than he. So he asked her if he could have her
permission to speak to her husband's attorney. She was
reluctant but grudgingly gave her consent. He also had to
ask her for the name of the attorney and where his office
was. She also supplied this information with bad grace.

As she was walking briskly to the door to see him out,
he stopped on the porch and asked, "Did you ever have a
worker named Mark Farleigh here before the war?"

"Do you honestly think I'd keep track of every itinerant who worked for a couple months that long ago? We've had dozens and dozens. Maybe hundreds."

The door slammed behind him.

When he'd introduced himself to the attorney's secretary, who was surprisingly young and pretty, but surly, he asked if he could see the will.

"That will be up to Mr. Woodly to discuss with you."

"I need to speak with him now," Walker said.

"I'll see if he's free to see you. I don't have you in my appointment book," she said, running a long, red, pointy fingernail down the page of the book in front of her.

When Howard was finally allowed to speak to the attorney, a plump individual sporting greased-back hair and a pin-striped suit that was a little too snug for his frame, the first thing the man said was, "Do you have a warrant?"

"No, but I can come back with one. Wills are filed as public documents anyway for probate, as you well know. You'd be better off showing it to me now than making me wait for the filing."

"I suppose so."

The will was short and said exactly what Mrs. Connor had reported.

"Did you draw this up?" Walker asked. "Your letter-head is on it."

"No, not precisely. Mr. Connor wrote it by hand. I just had my secretary correct the spelling and type it."

"Did you advise him?"

"I tried to. But he insisted he wanted to keep it precisely the way it was. It was foolish, not to say wicked. But he got what he paid for and wouldn't hear my reasoning."

"Which was?"

"That his grandsons might not be suitable heirs, since neither one had seen or spoken to him since they were children. When you're the local attorney, you know these things."

Walker didn't feel he was responsible for correcting this error and telling Mr. Woodly about Kelly Connor's visits.

"Have you contacted the grandsons about this?"

"No. I can't find either of them. The older one took a job in New York City, I'm told. And the younger, I hear, drives a bus around selling domestic items."

Walker rose from the highly uncomfortable chair clients had to sit in and thanked Mr. Woodly for his help and headed back to Voorburg, disappointed. He'd liked Miss Twibell's theory that the will was forged. There was no indication from Woodly that this was true. But he'd still keep the idea in his mind for future reference.

In fact, he wasn't sure he could believe anything he'd been told today.

As he was driving back, he thought of one more question he should have asked Miss Twibell and headed for the nursing home.

"I forgot to note the date the will was signed. Was it after Sean Connor's grandson Kelly started visiting him?" he asked her.

"Let me think. It was a very busy day, as I recall. I had a fifth patient who had just come in with a very bad abscess on his leg that required several lancings over a period of several days. Kelly Connor only came to visit later, I think. But I'll check my records and get back to you. I think Kelly's visits, the extra patient, and the lawyer's visit were fairly close together."

Lily had finished the last mopping of the day, and Robert had taken down the last load of laundry. Miss Twibell said they could leave early if they wished.

"I'd like to stick around, if you don't mind," Robert said. "I could help the Harbinger boys get the dumbwaiter working."

"So I have to walk home?" Lily said. "It's raining, in case you didn't notice."

"I'll drive you home, Lily," Howard volunteered.

Lily thanked him, and they walked out to his car together.

"Mind if we take the long way back? I'd like to talk to

you," Howard asked as he opened the door of the police car for her.

"Why not. And what have you learned about Mr. Connor's death?" Lily asked.

"I've been told quite a lot. But I don't believe most of what I've heard. You probably know about Mrs. Connor's rant about the will?"

"I think everybody in the nursing home heard it."

"When I went to speak to her," Howard said, "she repeated it word for word. It didn't sound real. Or rather, it seemed to be something she'd practiced saying for some time. A version of the property exchange that made her look saintly."

"I don't think either of them were ever the least bit saintly," Lily said.

"Neither do I," Howard replied, settling into the driver's seat. But instead of starting the car, he turned to face her. "And my conversation with Sean Connor's attorney was a waste of time. He went all saintly as well. He said it was all the old man's idea, and that he tried to talk him out of leaving the farm to the grandsons. I didn't believe him either. The only thing I learned from him, which he must have heard from Mrs. Connor, was that neither of the grandsons had any contact with their grandparents since they were small children."

"But Kelly visited his grandfather."

"That's the point. Nobody but the people at the nursing home seem to know about that. There's another thing that puzzles me," Howard said. "Miss Twibell told me what Mrs. Connor said here. And Mrs. Connor repeated it to me word for word, but she added something to it that might be the only true remark she made."

"What was that?"

"That she was hoping her husband would get well and go back to taking care of the farm. She's lost all her workers except one, and he's threatening to leave because he can't do everything. The crops should be planted soon or there won't be anything to grow and sell in the fall."

"Maybe this crossed her mind after she'd been at the nursing home," Lily speculated.

"It should have been the first thing she thought of, since she'd already driven away two of her farmhands with her overbearing attitude. The point is, if she did realize she needed him back, she's no longer a valid suspect."

Lily thought for a moment. "So Sean Connor died sometime after Kelly left. Or maybe before he arrived. Or maybe Kelly smothered him."

"Yes. Betty's admitted she just opened the door and looked at him after Kelly left. He might have already been murdered."

"But why would Kelly kill him? How could he have known about the will leaving the farm to him and his brother?"

"Only two ways," Howard said. "Either the attorney or

the secretary who typed it up blabbed to someone who told him."

"And both of them would lie if you asked them."

"True," Howard admitted. "And there's no way I could prove it. I'm sick to death of this case. But it's clear that Sean Connor was murdered, and I can't just throw my hands up and say I can't solve it. It's my responsibility to find out who smothered a nasty old man who was going to die that day anyway."

CHAPTER EIGHTEEN

So you didn't get anything helpful when you were in Beacon?" Lily asked.

"Not the second time," Howard replied, finally starting the car and heading back toward Grace and Favor.

"When were you there twice, and why?"

"It's nothing to do with the Connors," Howard explained.

"How do you know that? They live there. Tell me why you were there twice."

Howard almost laughed. "I hardly know where to start. I guess with the lake. It's the nastiest lake you've ever seen or smelled. Somehow a crevasse or long, skinny sinkhole opened up and rain filled it. So it doesn't have anything but rainwater coming in, and nothing going out except by evaporation. It's green and stinks."

He went on, "There's a really dotty old woman who lives nearby."

"Why would anyone live near it?"

"God only knows. There's a theory that she's dotty *because* of the smell."

"Nobody goes crazy because of a smell, do they?" Lily asked.

"They do if it's mustard gas. And the smell of the lake is nearly as bad, I'd guess. Although I've never had a whiff of it."

"So how do you know this, and why did you go there?" Lily asked.

"Because a young man drowned there sometime last winter. He was preparing to go ice-skating, and somebody shot at him, and he went headfirst and broke through the ice. He recently floated up to the top when the ice melted."

"Who was he?"

"Nobody knows. I don't mean to be indelicate, but he wasn't recognizable after a winter in that water. All we know is that he only had one skate on."

"Didn't this crazy woman see it happen?"

"That's debatable. She says she called the police because a mysterious hiker told her to. She says she knew that he was a Communist because he had a big stick, long dirty hair, and a red beret."

"Howard, are you making this up as you go just to entertain me?"

"I haven't got a weird enough imagination to invent

this. The crazy woman has a phone line, of all things, because there are a group of men who fish there. . . ."

"Oh, ick! They must be nasty fish!"

"Probably. Maybe some of them have turned into evolutionary throwbacks. Maybe that's why the men fish there," Howard said, smiling. "Could be they're selling them to freak museums."

"You're getting away from the point again. How did you end up going there?"

"I was helping out a fellow chief of police up there who's laid up with gout and has a brand-new deputy. So I spent Sunday interviewing people who live in the hills around the stinky lake. Since none of them had seen anything, in desperation I took the new deputy along to interview the woman who lives near the lake. She has about a thousand cats, the logs are chinked with newspaper, and she claimed not to know a thing about it until a bunch of police from nearby towns arrived to remove the body."

"But she had reported it? Didn't you say that?"

"Yes, there's a record of her calling, but she denies it."

Lily thought for a while. "Could she have shot him herself, and made it up about being told about it?"

"Maybe. But I actually went into her so-called house and saw no evidence of a weapon of any kind except a rusty hatchet she must use to get firewood in the winter. By the way, she also reported a bear that tore down her storage shed and carried it away. The bear, she claimed, left behind his pry bar and some ropes."

"Now I *know* you're making this up!"

"No, I'm not. She did. And the police officer who grudgingly went to see her, saw them."

"So, where does this case stand right now? Will they ever find out who the young man is?"

"I suggested to the Beacon chief of police that he should research when the ice might have been in a condition that a young man might fall through, and put a notice in the paper about any young man who went missing at that time."

"And has he had any response?"

"Not that I know of. If he had, he'd probably have called me back. It's not my case. I was just trying to help out until he was back on his feet."

"If you learn any more about this, will you tell me?"

"I suppose so. Why are you interested?"

"Just because it's such a bizarre story. May I share it with Robert?"

"He won't believe it either," Walker said as he drove by the gatehouse and up the driveway to Grace and Favor and dropped her off.

Robert was late coming home. Mrs. Prinney had to put his dinner in the oven to keep it warm. He looked exhausted and was covered with fine dark dust. His fingernails were broken and grimy, his fingertips red and swollen.

"It was really hard to take out that wall between the kitchen and the laundry," he whimpered to Lily while she sat with him as he ate. "And it made a real mess. I was the mess cleaner-upper. But they're ready to install the final parts tomorrow. I can't wait to see how it works."

He picked at his meat loaf for a minute, almost too tired to eat. "It's a scary hole right now, going down two whole stories. I think we're about to lose our job. Miss Twibell's feet are finally feeling better, and she's letting Mattie go home tomorrow or the next day to rest up for a few more days. She won't need us then. But I'm going to hang around anyway until I get to use the silent butler."

"I won't mind being replaced," Lily said. "It was probably the most physical work I've ever done in my life. I'll miss the money, though."

"We'll find something else to do. We're learning to do lots of things we've never done before."

"I have something interesting to tell you," Lily said. "A story Howard told me as he brought me home. He made a trip to Beacon on Sunday to help out another chief of police who couldn't get out of his house because of gout." She went on to explain about the nasty lake and the body that had floated to the top. Since Robert was still eating, she left out the most disgusting parts. But when she got to the houseful of cats and the bear that took away the old woman's shed and left behind his pry bar and some rope, Robert nearly choked on his coffee.

"That's the funniest thing I've ever heard," he said when he finished coughing. "Are you certain he didn't make that up?"

"He swore it was what she told the local police."

Then Lily went on to explain how frustrated Howard was in his investigation of Sean Connor's death, and his feeling that the responses he'd gotten from both the Beacon attorney and Mrs. Connor were so well rehearsed.

She continued, "He also said Mrs. Connor, who was his best suspect, had added to her story that she'd lost all but one of the workers and he would probably be leaving, too. She was hoping, she told Howard, that Mr. Connor would recover and come back and see that the crops were planted."

"Connor really left the land to the grandsons?" Robert asked. "Why would he have done that?"

"Nobody knows. Pure spite is my guess. Miss Twibell rashly suggested that Mrs. Connor get another attorney to overrule the will. Then regretted getting involved."

"I think Miss Twibell was right," Robert said.

He thought for a moment and said, "If the loony old woman didn't see the floating body, who did?"

"That's where the Communist comes in," Lily explained. "According to her phone call to the police—which she later denied to Howard—the Communist was hiking near her house back in December and saw the body go in the lake. He ran down the hill to ask if she could call the police, which she did. Then he disappeared. The dotty old woman said he was a Communist, coming to grab her and take her to Russia. He had a stick, long greasy hair, and wore a red beret."

"He was probably just a hiker, don't you think?" Robert asked.

"If he existed at all," Lily replied. "There is that bear story she told."

"Don't you think it's interesting that the Connors are from Beacon and so is this mysterious body?"

Lily pondered this. "I can't see a connection."

"Neither can I. But it is odd."

Lily's thoughts strayed. "I wonder if Kelly Connor knows his grandfather is dead."

"Maybe," Robert said. "He might be the killer himself."

"I simply can't believe that. You didn't meet him. I did. He was such a cheerful young man. And he seemed honest. When he was showing us his products, he even mentioned that he thought one was overpriced."

"What product?"

"I don't remember. But I still don't think he'd hurt anyone. I fancy that I have an instinct about who's nice and who isn't."

"Most people think that, too. I mean, about themselves. The fact is, if the will says what Mrs. Connor says it does, your nice young man with the trinkets inherits half of his grandfather's farm, and there's been no sign of him at the nursing home since his grandfather's death."

"Maybe he's just been in other towns," Lily argued. "It's not that he visited every week. Just when he was in Voorburg. He will be back. Mrs. Prinney wanted galoshes that he had to order specially by color and size."

"What about the other brother?" Robert asked. His eyelids were getting heavy, and when Mimi brought in a dessert for him, he turned it down.

When Mimi had gone, Lily said, "Nobody seems to know anything about where he is. He had a job in New York City working on one of those skyscrapers."

"Can't the New York City police ask around for him?"

"I think they probably have too many other things to deal with," Lily answered. "But I'll ask Howard about it the next time I see him. I'm sure that's something he's thought of. Go take a bath and go to bed, Robert."

CHAPTER NINETEEN

On Tuesday, the Harbinger boys started assembling the working parts of the dumbwaiter. Robert had his hopes up that this was the day the food might come up and the dirty dishes go down without anyone having to carry them. The kitchen skivvy hoped so, too. But Robert was most concerned about the laundry. He was sick and tired of hauling it up and down two flights of stairs.

But it wasn't to be. When the trial run with just the ropes was being done, the platform stuck at the first-floor level. Apparently it had swung a mere quarter inch to one side and got caught under what used to be the extra bathroom on the first floor. It took the Harbinger boys a half hour to make a slightly bigger cut in the shaft, and while they were doing so, they decided the platform needed to go up and down on a track of some sort so that it couldn't sway in the vertical column and get trapped between floors.

Harry Harbinger was furious with himself when he

realized that his one experience with the workings of an elevator years ago had been missing one important element. They had to take new measurements and go back to Poughkeepsie. They didn't have much confidence that an ordinary hardware store would have elevator tracks. What's more, if they had to order them, the expense would be horrendous, and a lot of time would be lost. Worst of all, they had no way to carry a three-story set of metal tracks and it would be impossible to bend them to run them up the chute.

For once in his life, Robert accidentally made a genuinely good suggestion. "Why don't you use wood instead of metal?"

"Because it would rub against the wood projecting from the platform," Harry said.

"Not if you greased the uprights and the projecting pieces that are on the platform that fit between the pieces of wood," Robert said.

The Harbinger boys started discussing what sort of grease it would take. Motor oil was too thin. Butter was too expensive and would soak in and go rancid and stink in the summer. They finally settled on a hard varnish, another expense, but not as impossible as metal. Then almost anything sufficiently oily could be poured sparsely down the tracks from the top whenever needed.

The most horrifying part of this was presenting the problem to Miss Twibell.

More practical than the men, she agreed to fund half the price of the wood and the varnish. But she insisted that any time the platform starting sticking, the Harbinger boys would supply and apply the extra oil at no cost to her.

Robert and Harry's brother didn't think this was fair, but didn't say so in front of Miss Twibell. And Harry, who took the whole blame for forgetting the rails, had already agreed to Miss Twibell's solution.

As he was seeing them off in their truck, Robert said, "Please hurry. I want to see this work. Though I don't think it's quite right you should lose some of your profit."

"It won't cost us much," Harry said. "But it will take more time, I'm sorry to say."

"But what if the two of you move away someday? Who's going to do it?"

"Move away from Voorburg?" Harry asked, astonished at the very thought. "We'll never move away. This is where we live." He gunned the engine of the truck and took off.

Robert realized with a sinking heart that he had at least several more days of hauling laundry up and down. Besides, he was stuck living in Voorburg for another eight years and could learn to oil the rails if the Harbinger boys happened to change their minds, marry girls from other towns, and move closer to their wives' families.

He also surprised himself by realizing that staying in Voorburg that long wasn't really all that bad. When he'd first come here, he'd hated it. Now he had friends here he'd miss desperately.

The days had lengthened enough that it was still barely light when he and Lily got off work and drove home. As the Duesie made the first of the many sharp turns going to Grace and Favor, Robert stopped the automobile abruptly when he spotted an odd-looking man who was about to disappear down one of the old Indian paths that led to the river. Robert tried to point the figure out to Lily.

"I don't know where you're looking," Lily said.

"He's already gone. I think it was that crazy woman's Communist. He had a big walking stick, long brown hair, and some sort of red hat. I'm going to follow him. Stay here in the car. I wish we had a way of calling Howard to tell him."

"Robert, if you can catch up with him, I'll drive the automobile to town and tell Howard."

In theory, this was a good plan, but Robert hated to turn the Duesie over to Lily. She'd driven it only a few times, and wasn't very good at turns. Time was of the essence though, so he reluctantly agreed and plunged into the woods, calling back to her as he departed, "Drive really slowly and carefully."

"Nonsense," Lily said to herself, climbing into the driver's seat.

She caught up with Howard at his boardinghouse as he was getting ready to sit down to dinner, and took him aside to explain who Robert thought he'd seen.

"Which path did he take?" Howard asked. "And where does it come out?"

"I don't know," Lily replied. "It was closer to the nursing home than to Grace and Favor. I've never followed it to town."

"Then you go to the icehouse and wait to see if that other path intersects with yours. I'll look around for where the other ones come down toward the river. Better yet, I'll drop you off and take the Duesie. If I approach him in the police car, I might scare him back into the woods if he's up to no good."

Lily didn't like this plan. It was getting dark now and the ice stored in the icehouse over the winter would be melting, making the area terribly muddy. Besides, the town icehouse was a sort of scary, remote place for a woman to be alone in the dark. But it was a sensible plan, so she went along with it, wishing there had been a flashlight in the Duesie she could use. That way, she could if the mysterious stranger Howard thought might be up to no good could be seen by her before he saw her.

She lingered around the side of the icehouse that faced the town, occasionally peeking around the corner at the path that came down the hill. She didn't hear anyone, so returned to the front for a while. Her shoes were getting clumped with mud. It was turning colder and she hadn't worn a warm enough coat.

Suddenly she heard what sounded like a branch being snapped back and became seriously frightened. She went a little closer to the corner but didn't peek around. Suddenly a person turned the corner and ran into her.

Both of them yelped with surprise and jumped back from each other.

"Lily? Is that you? What the hell are you doing here? Where's the Duesie?"

Robert was covered with burrs and had leaves and twigs in his hair.

"You frightened me nearly out of my mind. And you look a wreck. Didn't you find him?"

"He disappeared before I could spot him. I could hear him but not see him, and I must have taken a wrong turn. I didn't know this path came out here. The only ones I know fairly well are the ones that run south from Grace and Favor." His voice was rising. "Where is the Duesie? Have you left it somewhere where anyone could steal it?"

"No. Howard's driving it to where the other paths come down to the river."

"You turned the Duesie over to Howard? How could you? He doesn't know how to drive it."

"He's a better driver than I am. And he didn't want to let the person see him driving the police car."

"So what do we do now?" Robert asked. "Walk back up that hill in the dark?"

"I don't know the way in the dark. I've only come this way a few times, and it was with Phoebe in the daytime."

"Well, let's just wait for Howard to come find us," Robert said.

There wasn't anywhere to sit down while they waited, except for a couple of stumps. Lily sacrificed one of her best handkerchiefs to put on the stump before sitting down. "I wonder when Howard will show up?" she said.

"We shouldn't be talking, Lily. The Communist hiker might hear us and run away."

"That would be all right with me," she said. "I didn't want to be involved in this anyway."

"Whisper. We should try to explain to Mrs. Prinney why we aren't home for dinner yet," Robert said. "It's turkey tonight."

"How do you intend to contact her from here?" Lily said sarcastically.

"I thought I might run over to Mabel's and ask to use her phone," Robert said.

"You're doing no such thing. If anyone is going to Mabel's, it will be me. I'm not sitting here alone again."

"Have it your way. And if you spot the Duesie, make Howard bring it back."

Lily felt vastly relieved to be out of the woods and in the village. She gave Mabel a pocketful of change and called home. "We're going to be a bit tardy, Mrs. Prinney. We had to help Chief Walker hunt for someone. The chief may be coming to dinner with us, if you don't mind."

"I put the turkey in the oven a little late anyway. That's fine," Mrs. Prinney replied.

As Lily headed back to the icehouse, Howard spotted her and drove her the rest of the way. "Did you find him?" she asked.

"Almost," he said. "I'll explain when we pick up Robert."

Robert was glad to have his automobile back. Lily told them both that the turkey had been put in late and wouldn't be dried out, and that Howard was invited to dinner.

"So, what did you mean that you 'almost' found the hiker?" she asked Howard as Robert drove the three of them up the hill.

"Close to the lower end of one of the paths, I could smell a campfire that had recently been put out with water. It's such a nasty distinct smell, you can't help but notice it. There wasn't anyone around that I could see or hear. I think he'd probably cooked up something for his dinner and gone farther into the woods to sleep overnight. It will be easier to find him in the morning. I'll roust out Ralph early in the morning, and see if his cousin Jack is available to help look in the area, too. Thanks for inviting me to dinner."

"I took Howard away from the boardinghouse just as dinner was about to be served," Lily explained to Robert.

"Thank you for that," Howard said. "The woman who cooks was just putting out tiny leathery pork chops, a huge stinking bowl of cabbage, and overcooked lima beans."

CHAPTER TWENTY

Wednesday, March 16

As it turned out, Chief Walker and his deputy, Ralph, didn't need to search the woods. They'd arrived at Mabel's very early for breakfast because it had rained overnight and turned colder. Walker thought going without food would make the situation even worse. But they found what appeared to be their quarry eating ham and eggs at a table at the back. It was a table for two, and Howard sat down across from the man, with Ralph standing behind him, and said, "I'm Chief of Police Walker and this is my deputy. We need to talk to you."

The man started to rise, preparing to bolt. Howard reached across the small table and put a firm hand on his shoulder. "You're not in trouble. We just need some information from you."

The man subsided. He had no choice. He wouldn't be able to force his way past both officers and the rest of the guests. "What information?"

"Who are you, and what are you doing in Voorburg?" Howard asked.

His quarry's reply verged on outraged arrogance, as if he were so well known that everybody should recognize him. "My name is Charley Atkinson. I'm an arithmetic teacher in Beacon. The children are all passing around chicken pox, so the school is closed this week. And I'm taking the week to do some hiking. It's what I always do on school vacations. Keeps me away from children. Not that it's any of your business."

"Were you hiking over Christmas vacation?"

"Yes, I was," he admitted, but still in a surly fashion. "But not far. It was too cold to camp out in the woods. I went to my boardinghouse every evening. What's wrong with that? Hiking keeps me strong and sane."

"There's nothing wrong with it, Mr. Atkinson. I think you were near that foul-smelling lake at some point, weren't you?"

"How did you know that?"

"I'll explain later, if you don't mind answering my questions first," Howard replied. "Why did you happen to choose to go there?"

"I hadn't ever been near it, but I'd heard of it and was curious about it. It was a terrible mistake. I saw something that will haunt me for a long time."

"You saw something that shocked you?"

"I sure did. I was on the hill above the lake." Now that

he no longer felt quite so threatened, he became gabby. "I spotted a young man putting on his ice skates sitting at the edge of the lake. I thought he might be one of my former students. I meant to go in a different direction to avoid him. But before I could even turn, I heard a loud noise and saw him catapult headfirst into the lake. I rushed down, hoping I could pull him out."

"Did you manage to?"

"No. The hill was steep. I kept falling in my rush to help. By the time I arrived, there was no sign of him. Only a big hole in the ice. If one person could go through the ice, so could I. Call me a coward if you want. I tried to get help for him though. I could see that there was a run-down house half concealed behind a small hill above the lake, and I noticed there was something strung up that looked as if it were a phone line. I thought I was imagining it at first. Why would a phone line run to such a remote place?"

"Strange, indeed. I'll explain that to you later, if you like," Howard said. "Please go on."

"I could see smoke coming out the bent stovepipe. I hoped someone was there. I tried to look in a window to get someone's attention, but the windows were all covered up with what looked like rags. So I just pounded on the door, and shouted to call the police several times. No one responded. But the rags over another window were briefly opened, so I was sure it was occupied."

"Did you see anyone else?" Howard asked.

"I did. There was a tall figure in black striding fast up the hill behind the horrible little house. I tried to follow, but my legs were shaking so badly from the shock of what I'd seen that I had no hope of catching up. I didn't want to shout. That might attract his attention."

"It was a man?" Howard asked.

"I assumed so. The person was quite tall—and frightening."

"In what way frightening?"

"He was all in black. Black boots. A long black coat. What looked to me like a black fur hat."

"Did the person ever turn back? Did he seem to suspect he was being followed?"

"He never turned back, so I couldn't see his face. Though, in my attempt to follow, I dislodged several rocks. He might have heard me thrashing along way behind him. Every time I made a noise, I tried to hide behind a tree or a rock."

"What did you do next?"

"I gave up. I was sick to my stomach and terribly upset. I went back the way I'd come and went to the boardinghouse."

"Why didn't you call the police then?"

Charley Atkinson didn't speak for a moment. He looked as if he might break into tears.

"I was afraid. Afraid that someone would think I was making it up and that the horrible children would hear about it and laugh at me. Or that the police would think I'd killed the boy by not trying to wade in and find him. I didn't want to be thought either crazy or a coward."

"If it makes you feel better, the boy was dead before you arrived. You couldn't have saved him if you'd tried. That noise you heard was a shotgun," Howard told him.

But Howard thought that not calling the police was where Charley had stepped over into cowardice. It might have been that it wasn't a phone line. Maybe even if it was, the phone could have no longer worked. Or the resident hadn't bothered to call? It had been Charley's duty to report what he'd seen, even if the children found out about it, and laughed at him. They probably already laughed at him anyway for the way he dressed and his long dirty hair.

Charley, having told his story, asked, "How do you know about this? And how did you recognize me as having anything to do with it?"

"You were described by the woman who lives in that house."

"How did she describe me?"

He's vain as well, Howard thought.

"As having longish brown hair and a red beret," Howard said, leaving out the rest of the description, which had characterized him as a Communist. "The reason the old woman has a phone line is that a bunch of men fish there in the summer—"

"There are fish in that putrid lake?" Charley interrupted.

"I suppose there are. That's the reason for the phone line. The men offered to pay for it so they could tell their wives and girlfriends when they'd be home."

"Did the police get the boy out of the lake?" Charley asked.

"Not until the ice broke up in the spring."

"Do you know who he was?"

"Nobody knows yet. But I'll give you some good advice, Charley. You better tell Chief of Police Simpson in Beacon everything you told me. I'm going to tell him anyway, but you'd be better off if you told him before I do. If you don't—I know where to find you."

Charley fumbled in his pocket for change and rose and walked to the front to pay his bill without another word.

Ralph sat down in Charley's chair. "What a sissy he is. All that long hair. The silly hat."

Walker said, "That's just a superficial description. He's also a coward. He had a duty to report to the police himself instead of leaving it to an invisible person."

Ralph looked longingly at all the food Charley had left on his plate. "You *are* going to call Chief Simpson right away, aren't you?" he asked.

"As soon as we've had our own breakfast, you bet I will. I want Simpson to know, before Charley can find a phone, what he said to us. Just so he doesn't leave something out of the version he told us. Still, finding him here was better than having to comb the woods all day. It's already starting to rain again."

Walker signaled to Mabel that she could take away the congealing eggs and ham and bring them the same, adding fried potatoes and strong coffee with lots of sugar.

"A tall man all in black?" Simpson asked. "With a black fur hat?"

"I don't know if he was tall. This Charley fella was pretty short. Maybe he thinks everybody else is tall," Howard said.

"The person in black sounds like someone who'd just been to a funeral. Did Charley say when he saw all this happen?"

"Not specifically. But he suggested it was when the kids he teaches were out for Christmas. By the way, have you received any tips from what you put in the local papers about a young man who's been missing?"

"Tons of them. Mostly from young women who can't read very well. One of them called yesterday and said her boyfriend disappeared last week. Another said hers ran off a month ago. I had made clear it was last winter."

"How's the gout?"

"Lots better. I can get my shoes on and keep 'em on for

two hours at a time before my toes start hurting again. How's your case going?"

"Slowly," Howard admitted.

The Harbinger boys turned up very early with a load of long, thin boards. "How can I help?" Robert asked eagerly. Mattie was ready to go home later that day and all her bedding, including the heavy waxed pad on the bed, had to go down to the laundry.

Harry Harbinger said, "We have to measure the platform indents at the top floor, then you can hold the plumb line on the marks we make."

Robert had no idea what a plumb line was, but if it was necessary, he'd be eager to hold it.

Holding it turned out to be the easy part. The plumb line was a strong, thin string with a heavy lead weight attached at the end. But when he looked down the shaft to see what the Harbingers were doing, he nearly fainted. Both of the younger men were bracing their feet against one side of the shaft and their backs against the other side and inching upward, using pencils to mark where the string hung. He was deeply sorry he'd looked down, especially when Harry yelled up, "Stop letting the string wobble!"

When they'd finally finished and inched their way back down, Robert went to the basement. A friend of the Harbingers had come along to varnish the sticks in the kitchen. He had most of them done, in spite of the cook's outrage at stinking the place up. "It's going to make lunch smell awful!" she claimed.

But the helper had said, "Miss Twibell wants us to hurry. It's raining outside, and too damp in the laundry room for them to dry."

The sticks were laid out on newspapers, and they did smell awful. But there were only four left to do.

"Can you finish today?" Robert asked in a pleading tone to Harry.

"Maybe," was Harry's answer.

CHAPTER TWENTY-ONE

Thursday, March 16

Chief of Police Simpson called Howard Walker early the next morning. "I have a lead on my body from the lake. I'd like your advice," Simpson said, sounding weary.

Howard wondered why Simpson, who had at least thirty more years of experience than he did, needed advice. Maybe the gout had kicked in again. Or maybe since he had made an attempt to help Simpson before, Simpson was thinking of Howard as a backup deputy.

"What did you learn? Walker asked.

"A young woman named Sue Ann Wayne wrote me a letter saying she's seen the article, and the person I was looking for might be Aidan Connor. He could be identified by a large mole on the inside of his left forearm. They were engaged to be married, but he'd left his home in late December to take a construction job in New York to make enough money to marry her. She thinks he said he was going to work on the construction of the Empire State Building."

"That's already completed, I believe," Howard said. "But he might have stayed on in some sort of maintenance capacity. Have you already contacted whoever did the autopsy to find if there was such a mole?"

"Yep. I did that. He said the body was too putrefied to determine if there was a mole, unless it was huge one. And they still wouldn't know if they exhumed it."

"Then I'd suggest that you talk to his father and mother about this mole, if you haven't already done so. Not that it would prove who it was. But you might learn from them just where this Aidan really is."

There was a long silence before Simpson said, "Thanks, Howard."

Howard hung up speculating that Simpson's apparent weakness wasn't just the result of gout. The man wasn't even thinking like a cop anymore. Maybe it was time for him to retire and turn things over to his deputy, young Parker.

Howard had taken the call at the jail. Neither of the two cells was occupied, and it was quiet enough to catch up on paperwork. But he was interrupted again in a few minutes.

A young man came through the door looking very upset. "Someone tried to set my truck on fire."

"Did they succeed?"

"No."

"Then sit down and calmly tell me about it. Who are you?"

"Kelly Connor. I have a truck—well, it's really a small enclosed bus. I take samples of things around to various towns, showing them to people, and then deliver what they order if I haven't got the full-sized one on the bus."

"I've heard of you. I'm Chief of Police Howard Walker, and I'm friends with the people who live at Grace and Favor. They told me about you." *And so have other people,* Howard thought to himself.

Kelly nodded. "Nice people, they are. I've been in so many other towns roundabouts that I haven't been able to get the full-size version of some of the things they ordered until yesterday. I drove up here last night but was too late to call on them."

"So, get back to telling me what happened."

"I parked my bus down by the riverside and went in search of food. The man at the greengrocer was taking in a late shipment of vegetables, and I managed to get something to eat and took it back to my truck in the rain. I could smell smoke. I looked all around and found the smell was coming from under my bus. Someone had piled some driftwood under the engine and set fire to it. It's a good thing it was raining. The wood was damp. The fire was still slightly hot and there were a few feeble embers that were red. I moved the bus as quick as I could. Then ran down to the river with a bucket and put the fire out."

"So the bus is all right?"

"Yes. It could have blown to smithereens though. I

want to know who would want to do that to me. I can imagine someone breaking into it to steal things. That's happened before. But why would anyone want to destroy it?"

"You fail to understand the thrill vandals get from destroying things for no reason," Walker replied.

"I don't think it was naughty little boys. I think somebody wanted my business to fail."

"Then why set a fire in the rain?"

"Maybe it was just a threat?" Kelly said.

"Do you have enemies?" Walker asked.

"Not exactly. Oh, there have been a few people I've called on and sold things to who didn't like the products as much as they thought they would. That's all."

"Okay. I'll ask around to see if anybody noticed strangers or even neighbors wandering around late last night. That's the best I can do. I'm glad the bus didn't blow up."

"Thank you, sir. I'll be around for a couple more days. I have a few deliveries to make, and then I'm going to visit my grandpa at the nursing home." He stood up to shake hands with Howard.

"What's your grandpa's name?" Walker asked, though he knew the answer. He'd hoped someone else could break the bad news and then he would question the young man afterwards. But here he sat, unawares. Might as well get it over with.

"Sean Connor, sir. He's laid up with an infected knee."

Walker said, "Sit back down, son. I'm afraid I have bad news for you."

"About my bus, you mean?"

"No. About your grandfather. I'm afraid you won't be seeing him. He died about ten days ago."

Kelly looked shocked. "Ten days ago? I think that might have been the last day I saw him."

"So I'm told," Walker said. "I'll need to ask you a few questions about that visit."

Kelly asked, "Could I make my deliveries first and come back here?"

"I'm afraid not. I'll need to talk to you now. It probably won't take long."

"Where is he buried?" Kelly asked.

"In the family plot on the farm land."

Kelly pointedly didn't comment. He just frowned.

Walker pulled out his file and rummaged around for a few minutes. "What time did you get to the nursing home to visit?"

Kelly was staring at the bulging file. "What's all that paperwork? And why are you asking me?" He was looking seriously distressed now instead of merely sad.

"Because he was murdered that morning," Walker told him. He hated saying this to the young man, but Kelly would eventually find it out. He might as well hear it now in private.

"Murdered!" Kelly said, leaping to his feet. "Who did it?"

"I don't know. That's why I need to talk to you about your visit."

"You don't think *I* did it. You *can't* think that! He was a tough old bird and rude to everyone. But he was my grandpa. The only one I had left."

"I'm sorry about that. It's why I need all the information you can give me." Howard didn't feel this was the time to tell Kelly that his rude grandpa had made a will giving him, and his brother, the farm his grandmother had inherited. That would color the questioning, and it wasn't Howard's responsibility.

"What time did you get to the nursing home that day?" Howard asked, gesturing that Kelly should sit back down.

"I dunno. It was real early," he said, all but collapsing into the chair. "It was one of the same days my grandmother usually visited. I never wanted to be there when she was. I guess it was around seven-thirty or eight. I took him some little samples and put them on the table beside the bed."

"Did he like them?"

Kelly shrugged. "I couldn't tell. He was sound asleep."

"You're sure of that?"

"He was snoring. He didn't wake up when I talked to him real quiet. But then, he never really talked to me anyway."

"What did you say to him when you visited?"

"Oh, just stuff about where I'd been. What the weather was like outside. People I'd met and whether they'd bought anything from me. He always pretended he was asleep. But sometimes when I made a joke, I could see his lips twitch a little."

"But not that day?"

"No. He was sound asleep."

"Thank you for answering my questions. I may have others to ask you. I hope you'll be in Voorburg for a few more days. I do regret that I had to give you the bad news."

Kelly left, looking distinctly downcast.

Howard leaned back in his chair and put his feet on the desk. It was his best thinking position, and now he thought about Kelly Connor. The young man was attractive, with his red hair and freckles. He was also personable. It was no wonder he was a good salesman. But Howard had no idea whether Kelly was telling the truth. Salesmen didn't always do so. In fact, some of them could lie charmingly. He was well-spoken, as well, but not *too* well-spoken. He wouldn't intimidate people less well educated. And Howard would bet that any household with young girls would end up buying a lot of things from him.

But Kelly had come into the jail building clearly upset about the fire under the engine of his bus. He wasn't selling anything, he was complaining. And now Howard wondered, was the fire a genuine attempt to blow up the bus, or just vandalism?

Some of the older schoolboys in and around Voorburg, having to work so much of the time for their family in these tough times, did go in for petty vandalism. They were probably boys who would have thought it was fun even in better times. However, it was usually painting something on a shop window or damaging something like a statue, which was offensive behavior, but not dangerous.

Setting a fire under a vehicle was a whole different thing. It was meant to harm a person or personal property. It could have blown the windows out of several shops near the riverfront or injured anyone who happened to be out late at night.

It could have blown up Kelly as well, if the wood hadn't been so damp and Kelly hadn't been out searching for something to eat.

He looked through his file on the Connor case one more time. The only result was to neaten it up. It led him to no conclusions he hadn't already considered. As he was putting it back in the desk, the phone rang again.

It was Miss Twibell, speaking softly. "Kelly Connor is here at the nursing home," she said.

"Why?"

"To thank us for taking care of his grandfather. Do you need to speak to him while he's in Voorburg?" Miss

Twibell asked. "I could keep him here on some pretense if you need me to."

"I've already had quite a long conversation with him," Howard said. "I don't believe he's going to bolt."

Howard set out to question the greengrocer to find out if he'd seen anyone else roaming around for no good reason last night.

The greengrocer wasn't helpful. "I was out back of the building helping to unload. I didn't see anyone, except that red-headed kid."

Just to make sure he'd done the best he could, Howard went around to the other merchants and asked them if they'd been in their shops late and had they seen anyone roaming the streets. All of them replied that they had worked a good long day, and gone home in time for dinner.

Howard went back to his office for one more perusal of the Connor file, and while he was doing so, the phone rang again.

"Chief Simpson here," the voice said.

Howard had to stifle a groan of irritation. "What have you learned?" he asked as politely as he could.

"Aidan Connor did have a small mole where the girl said it was. But he isn't exactly missing. Three or four weeks ago, Stefan and his wife had a letter from a hospital in the city, typed by a nurse, informing them that their son had broken his right wrist and couldn't write for himself. She assured them he was in no danger and was healing well, and he'd write to them again as soon as he could."

"Did they visit him at the hospital?" Howard asked.

"No, they said they were too busy to leave their business. It's a gasoline station, and if nobody is there, they'd lose money. They said that if the report had suggested that their son was in any danger, they'd have immediately made the trip."

Howard had vowed not to give any more advice. He broke the vow. "Did they keep the letter?"

"Yes. They showed it to me."

"Did you look in a New York phone book to see if there *is* such a hospital?"

After a long silence, "I didn't think there was any need to. Do you think there's something suspicious about this letter?"

"Probably not. But I'd have checked its origin. And I'd probably ask them to keep the letter until they hear again from their son. But it's up to you. It's your case, not mine."

When he'd hung up, he stomped out of the office, hoping he could keep away from phones for the rest of the day.

CHAPTER TWENTY-TWO

Friday, March 17

Howard was wide awake at five the next morning. He'd had a nightmare that woke him up sweating and breathless. In the dream, he was on a bus that was on fire and floating down the Hudson River. The whole Connor family was on it with him—including dozens of relatives he'd never met or seen or even known about. They didn't seem to notice the fire or that they were probably going to drown.

Since he was already wide awake, he went to his office at the jail to go over his notes again. He'd have breakfast as soon as Mabel opened for business.

Howard felt as if he were surrounded by Connors. Whether working or eating or sleeping, he was constantly thinking about them. One murdered, one possibly missing, a third threatened by fire. And there was Mrs. Connor, a woman he hoped he'd never see again. But only one of them was his problem—Sean Connor, the old, sick, nasty man who'd been murdered on the same day he was fully expected to expire of natural causes.

It still made no sense at all. Why not just wait for him to die? Why would someone need to risk being arrested for smothering him? Why not sit it out at his bedside?

At least two other members of the Connor family might have been responsible for his death. His wife and his grandson Kelly. Mrs. Connor could have simply become sick and tired of visiting her husband and being ignored. Or she could well be telling the truth about needing him back to get the crops in. For a family that lived by what they grew and sold, this was vital.

Then there was Kelly Connor. He'd been threatened himself by someone who'd tried to blow up his bus. That vehicle was just as vital to the way Kelly made his own living. What's more, might that someone had reason to believe he was in the bus, and have been trying to kill him? Kelly appeared to be an ambitious young man. But he'd been the next to last person to see Sean Connor. He could have smothered his grandfather. But again, why? He had no reason, as far as Howard knew, to kill Sean. But Howard had only Kelly's word that his grandfather had been snoring. Nobody else had reported him snoring.

But what if Kelly had heard about the will leaving him and his older brother the Connor farm? This was unlikely, though, since the only way he could have come by this information was through the lawyer or the lawyer's secretary. Neither of them would have a clear motive to tell him. Or would they? What if the lawyer had wanted to keep the Connor family in his stable of clients? He'd never admit it, no matter how much pressure Howard exerted.

There were still other suspects. Betty had borne the brunt of taking care of Sean Connor for his final days. It could be that the old man attacked her with his last bit of strength and she retaliated. Or he said something so nasty to her that she couldn't bear to ever go in his room again. Except to smother him.

The shell-shocked Mark Farleigh was still on his list as well. He seemed a thoroughly nice person. But other soldiers who'd suffered in the Great War had brooded for years over the experience and then suddenly snapped into murderous rages. It was highly unlikely Howard could even interview Farleigh. It seemed the only person he ever spoke to since the war was Miss Twibell. And then seldom and only to reply to her, never to start a conversation on his own. The rest of the patients and staff believed he was truly mute.

Practically anyone else, except Miss Jones and Miss Smith, could have done it if they'd been fit enough. Miss Jones would have run out of breath. Miss Smith wouldn't be able to let go of her sticks.

It was possible, as well, that someone nobody even knew about had been in the nursing home and held a deep grudge against Sean Connor. There were brief times, Howard supposed, when no one was in the main room and someone could have sneaked in between the other visitors. Miss Twibell, for all her good intentions, wasn't very good about making sure all the doors were always locked.

Supposing one of his neighboring farmers had been negotiating with Sean Connor to buy out his farm and was tired of waiting for the old man to die? It was the time to be preparing the soil for crops. If such a person wanted to farm it this year, he wouldn't be able to if Mr. Connor hung on much longer.

Miss Twibell had said that some of his farm neighbors had visited him once. They'd know which room he was in. One or the other of them might have lurked around when the door was unlocked, and watched from some hiding place to see where everyone was, and committed the murder, not even aware that Sean had only a few hours left to live.

There was always the wandering-maniac theory to fall back on as well, but he wouldn't even bother considering this.

Too much time was passing without his coming up with any believable motives that he could prove without a doubt.

Much as he'd like to simply give up, he couldn't. A man had been murdered. It was his job to find out why, and by whom. It was one of the many things he was being paid to do.

He finally admitted to himself that he'd have to start from scratch. He might not have asked the right questions of the right people, or been as aggressive as he should have been.

He had rushed and tried to question everyone as soon as he could. That was probably a mistake. He made notes of those he had to go back to, and what he needed to say to force them to cough up the truth. That was part of the problem with this case. There were too many people he felt hadn't told him the truth. Just the parts of the truth they were willing to reveal.

At nine-thirty in the morning the dumbwaiter butler was finally in operation. Robert was thrilled. He insisted on being the first one to actually use it. He loaded it up with the breakfast plates and sent it down to the basement. He was astonished that the ropes were so easy to operate. But he was afraid that with a significant weight, he might lose his grip on the rope and all the dishes and glasses would end up in shards.

"Miss Twibell, you'll want to try this yourself before the Harbingers hook it up to the electricity. It's much easier than you think," he told her. "But you might ask them to put some sort of bell at the top and bottom in case nobody hears it come down. It makes almost no sound at all, and someone either up here or in the basement might not notice it had arrived."

"That's a good idea. And running it without electricity would save me some money," she said. "It's a practical thought."

Robert wondered why she thought his having a practical thought was noteworthy.

"Why don't you call down to the laundry and ask Doreen to send up whatever bedding she has ready, and we'll find out if it comes up as easily as it goes down," he suggested.

She did so, and the dumbwaiter sent up a heavy load without any strain on the rope at all. "I'm delighted!" Miss Twibell gushed. "I'm so glad you talked me into doing this—it will save so much time and work for everyone. I wouldn't have believed it would be so easy to use. I'm calling Doreen again to see if it works this well sending the load back down."

"Want me to run down there and find out for you? And I'll also suggest the bell idea to the Harbinger boys. That should be easy to do."

"Would you, please?" Though her feet were finally feeling much better, she was grateful for the convenience of the dumbwaiter. It was never a joy, painful feet or not, to walk up and down two long flights of stairs.

Everybody who worked at the nursing home wanted to try out the silent butler. The laundry made a trip back down for Lily, and up again so Betty could experiment with it as well. They were all surprised and pleased at how easily and silently it glided along the tracks.

The cook, who had been observing in the basement, actually climbed both sets of stairs to tell Miss Twibell how grand it was. She was close to tears of gratitude. "Even knowing I'll probably never see you again except for payday," she said with a sappy smile.

When everyone had mastered the ropes, Miss Twibell said privately to Robert and Lily, "I'm sorry to say this, but we won't need you anymore. Mattie will be back soon, and Betty will have more free time to clean the floors and cabinets now that she and Mattie don't have to hand-carry the laundry. But Robert, since it was your idea, I'm giving you an extra bonus in your payment. Would half of what it would have cost to wire it for electricity be acceptable?"

"More than acceptable. It's very generous. I was feeling a bit guilty about forcing you to invest in this," he said. "Oh, I almost forgot to tell you, the Harbinger boys say the bells will be easy. They're already on their way to buy two of them."

As Robert drove Lily home a few minutes later, Lily said, "We're out of work again. What shall we do next? And don't say 'Listen to the radio,' or I'll go mad."

"You don't have to listen. I just want to keep up with what Roosevelt is doing."

"We might be able to help out Howard," Lily said. "He

seems to have become a bit cranky about this investigation of Mr. Connor's death."

"Has he asked for our help?"

"Have you already forgotten about trying to help him find that hiker?" Lily remarked.

"He didn't ask us to. We volunteered when I spotted the fellow in the woods."

"So what's wrong with us offering to help again?"

"I don't know," Robert admitted. "Somehow it's different. I don't think he's going to like us offering help."

"But he offered to help you take down those cabinet doors."

"That doesn't count. It wasn't something I was supposed to know how to do."

Robert was right.

Howard asked, "What makes you think I need help?" sounding offended.

Robert tried to make it seem like a joke. "Because we've been fired from our own jobs, and we're easily bored."

That made Howard smile slightly. "If I can think of anything you can do, I'll let you know. In fact, I'll let you read all my notes of the interviews I've done so far. Since both of you are such snoops, maybe you'll see something

I've overlooked. But I'm not letting them out of my sight. You have to read them here."

"Only if you make us a big pot of real coffee instead of that awful half-chicory stuff Mrs. Prinney insists on serving us," Lily said.

"By the way, Ralph and I didn't have to search the woods for the hiker. We found him eating breakfast at Mabel's," Howard told them.

"Did you get any valuable information from him?" Lily asked.

"Some. He saw a tall man, all in black, wearing a black fur hat, striding up the hill behind the loony woman's house."

Lily and Robert sat down and divided up the large file, trading off sections. Each made a few notes while Howard went to Mabel's to pick up sandwiches for the three of them. He was gone long enough for Lily and Robert to go through about two-thirds of the file.

When he returned, Lily said, "I had no idea you wrote down all this. Are you sure you remembered the exact wording the people used?"

"I have a good memory, and I always try to write it down before I even leave wherever I've been."

"There's only one thing I've seen so far that might not have been done," Robert put in. "But I haven't read it all yet. Did you find out from Miss Twibell the order in which the supposed lawyer asked her and Betty to sign as witnesses and when Kelly Connor started visiting his grandfather?"

Howard was ashamed to admit that he'd forgotten to check this. And apparently so had Miss Twibell. "I'll remind her today."

"I admit I'm a snoop and a cynic," Lily said, "but you're much kinder than I am. For example, you seem to believe Kelly Connor's story about someone trying to burn up his bus. I think it's probably true, but I'd go look under where the bus was parked just in case."

Howard grinned. "I did. He'd moved it away from the fire, but the tire tracks were there, and deeper where it had stood. The pitiful attempt to build a fire with damp driftwood and a few bits of loose lumber was obvious."

"Maybe you're not as nice as I feared," Lily said. "But could he have done it himself?"

"Why would he?" Robert asked.

Lily shrugged. "Who could tell? Maybe he has some secret of his own that required it."

"You know I can't take anyone to jail or court based on vague personal theories," Howard said. "I need hard evidence or a confession. But I can go and ask more questions."

"Who are the people you're going to question again?" Robert asked.

Howard listed them. "Betty at the nursing home. I need

to know more about how he reacted to her cleaning out his wound. It must have been painful, and he wasn't a pleasant person.

"I also need to put more pressure on Connor's attorney and his secretary. I need to know whether either of them talked to anyone else about the will. Even if they didn't name names. Could someone else have gossiped about it? My own impression of that girl wasn't flattering. She might have thought the will was so interesting that she shared the information with her girlfriends or boyfriends," Howard groused. "She's probably unaware, or doesn't care, that it's confidential until the writer of the will is dead.

"And I certainly don't believe much of what Mrs. Connor said. After she went after Miss Twibell and Betty about witnessing the will, and was finally convinced they truly didn't know it was a will, she fell apart and confessed all sorts of sappy personal information to them. But she added a practical note about needing to get the crops in when I questioned her."

"Even I would think about that first," Robert said.

Lily thought for a moment, then said, "Mrs. Connor doesn't like men. She didn't like her husband, her son, or either of her grandsons. But she poured out her story to two women. Maybe you could come up with some excuse for me to visit her on a purely social level. Though I can't imagine how I could butt in without making her angry. I wouldn't like to do it, but I would if it could provide you with more information."

Howard considered this. "You might be right about her attitude toward men. I'll try to think of some reason for your visiting her. Have all her husband's clothes and belongings been returned to her?"

"I have no idea," Lily said.

"I'll ask Miss Twibell about this, too. It might provide another thing to ask when I call on her. Inquire if anything was left behind. Though I doubt it. Although . . . if I explained why I need it, she might go along with 'finding' something that she mistakenly thought belonged to him and send you to deliver it."

Robert was still looking through some of the paperwork. "It's interesting what the hiker said about the man he saw going up the hill after the boy fell in the lake. Did you believe him?"

Howard thought for a moment. "I think he's the only person even remotely involved in Chief Simpson's case who really told the truth. But it's not my case, so it doesn't matter what I think."

As he was saying this, the phone rang. It was Chief Simpson. "Howard, I've checked. There isn't and hasn't ever been such a hospital."

Howard said, "Don't say anything else. Your telephone girl or mine might be listening. Wait just a minute."

He thought of an innocuous wording and said, "Go back to the people with the letter and bring a fresh envelope. Take the letter by the corner, put it in the envelope, and send your deputy with it to the fingerprint expert in Newburgh. Then you get a warrant for a typewriter, and any other objects that might be relevant to a murder case, and meet me at your office. I'll have two other people with me."

Simpson replied, "I think I know what you're getting at. I'll meet you in an hour."

CHAPTER TWENTY-THREE

I need you two to go along with me," Howard said.

"What is all this about?"

"I'll tell you on the way to Beacon. First we have to go to the nursing home."

Howard left them in the police car while he consulted with Miss Twibell. "I need something you can claim you just found that you think someone gave Mr. Connor early in his stay."

"What sort of thing?"

"I don't know. Maybe a book or a magazine?"

"He wasn't a reader. If that's what you need, though, someone gave me a book not long ago about learning how to play bridge. Would that do?"

"Perfect. They didn't inscribe it to you, did they?"

She went to fetch it and they checked. It wasn't inscribed to anyone.

Back in the police car, he started toward Beacon and

explained to the Brewsters what he thought and what roles they were to play.

Howard said, "Lily was right about something important."

When they reached Beacon, Chief Simpson had several warrants in hand, and Deputy Parker was back from Newburgh. Introductions were made, then Howard laid out the plan, concluding by saying to Simpson, "Follow me in your car, and bring Parker along. He needs the experience. We'll want to park out of sight and send Miss Brewster to the door with the book."

When they arrived at their destination, automobiles were parked down the lane leading to the house they were seeking. They all got out of the vehicles to confer, and Chief Simpson said, "What's going on here? Is it a St. Patrick's Day party or something?"

"God only knows," Howard said. "But we need to proceed. Lily, do you have the book? Remember to be the Queen of Sympathy no matter what that woman says."

"I'll do my best," she said, hurrying to the house.

As she approached, she noticed a handful of men in and around the barn removing tools and putting them in their trucks. The front door was open, and there was the sound of a mob of women talking somewhere. Lily stepped through into the main room just as Mrs. Connor came out of another where the voices were coming from.

Boxes and bags were piled everywhere in the main

room—on the big table with so many chairs, on sofas and side tables. Some had clothing in them; a few had toasters; others contained dishcloths, pots, meat pounders, sets of knives, or silverware.

"I'm so sorry to interrupt you," Lily said and introduced herself. "And sorrier yet about your husband's death and the rest of your troubles."

"I remember you, Miss Brewster. You and that Betty girl were so kind to me at the nursing home."

"Miss Twibell sent me to bring a book she just found in your husband's room at the nursing home that someone had given him as a gift. She sends her deepest apologies for not finding it sooner."

She handed the book to Mrs. Connor. While the woman was looking at it, Lily furtively glanced around and spotted a heavy-looking typewriter at the far end of the room, and something else that almost took her breath away.

"Why would someone have given my husband a book, Miss Brewster?" Mrs. Connor asked. "He never read anything, not even a newspaper. I'll give it to someone here. These people are the women in my own family."

She apparently had no sense of how much Lily was disliking chatting with her.

"What are the boxes and bags for, if you don't mind me asking?" Lily inquired.

"I'm moving out. A second cousin of mine is the president of a company and wants to buy my house for a great deal of money, and use it as a place to have meetings with his distributors. He has a lot more money than he deserves, and I don't mind taking it. He doesn't want anything but the big table and the chairs. I'm giving all the rest of the furnishings, except my personal belongings, to my relatives, including everything in the barn."

Then she added with a malicious glint in her eyes, "If my grandsons are getting the farm, they're going to have to come up with the money to buy new equipment to farm it."

Remembering Howard's admonition to be nice whatever Mrs. Connor said, even though Lily wanted to slap the woman for her nastiness, she said, "Where are you moving? Somewhere nice, I hope." Lily was sensing that this horrible woman enjoyed telling a younger woman all about herself, and all about how clever and how fortunate she was.

"It's a wonderful place. Another cousin of mine told me about a very exclusive boardinghouse near Poughkeepsie where a woman takes in widows of a good class. It has all the amenities. I visited it yesterday and looked at a suite that's been vacated. A lovely parlor, a big bedroom, and my own bath."

"How nice for you," Lily said. "Is the food good? Is that why you're giving away your kitchen things?"

"Yes. I had a meal while I was there. It was excellent. I'm sorry you took the time to bring the book. It was nice of you, but I don't want it. Maybe one of my cousins will."

"I see you have a typewriter. Are you giving that away, too?"

"Yes."

"May I buy it instead? I've been longing to learn how to typewrite, but can't afford a new one."

That made Mrs. Connor even more pleased. "What could you pay?"

"Five dollars?"

"Ten," Mrs. Connor countered.

Lily took out her billfold, pulled out her money, and showed it to Mrs. Connor. "I only have eight and a half dollars. Could I bring you the other dollar and a half later?" Five dollars of Lily's money had come from Mrs. Prinney, who had given it to her to pick up things from the greengrocer and the butcher. The rest was her own. Mrs. Prinney would understand when she was told why the grocery money had disappeared.

"I'll just take the eight and a half now, and call it a deal. I don't expect to be here much longer, I don't want to have to wait for you to come back with the rest of the money. So it's yours. You're too frail to carry it though. I'll have one of the men take it to your automobile."

This horrified Lily. The car she'd come in was a police car. She didn't want any of these people knowing that.

"Oh, no thank you. If you're strong enough, could we manage to scoot it along to the front porch? My brother's waiting for me, and he can carry it the rest of the way."

"Scooting would make marks on the floor," Mrs. Connor said as she put the top of the case on the typewriter and hefted it up as if it weighed nothing. She set it on the porch and went back into the house, thanking Lily once more for the book.

Lily was seething. She wanted to run away from this dreadful greedy woman, but forced herself to walk instead. The four men leaped out as she appeared in the shrub-shaded lane.

"Was there a typewriter?" Howard asked.

"Yes. I had to *buy* it. She's selling the house, moving into a grand boardinghouse, and giving her relatives everything else in it. The typewriter is sitting on the porch. Robert needs to come back with me to pick it up. And I saw something else."

She told them where and what it was.

As she and Robert walked back, she told him, "Pick up the case from front to back. She carried it out from side to side and her fingerprints will be on the bottom."

When the typewriter had been put in Chief Simpson's police car upside down to protect the prints, and speeded away to Newburgh, Howard said to Lily and Robert, "Stay here. I need to go in myself, and don't want her to see you two again. I'll take Parker along."

The front door was ajar, but he knocked. A big strong woman with coloring and features much like Mrs. Connor's came to the door. He asked if he could come in and speak to Mrs. Connor. The woman opened the door and disappeared into the kitchen.

Mrs. Connor emerged a moment later. "What are you doing here again!" she exclaimed.

"I think you'll want to discuss what I want quietly in the parlor, without eavesdroppers."

She simply glared at him, and then led him and Ron into the parlor.

Howard said, "I have a warrant for your arrest for the murder of your husband, the murder of your grandson Aidan, and the attempted murder of your grandson Kelly. I also have a warrant to take out anything relevant to these crimes from this house. I can handcuff you and take you away in a police car in plain view of your relatives. Or you can stay quietly under house arrest until they're gone. Which will it be?"

Ron was watching Mrs. Connor eagerly. He'd had only one chance to handcuff someone and was looking forward to doing it again.

For a brief moment Mrs. Connor looked surprised, then started hissing threats of lawsuits and proclaiming her complete innocence of the charges, all interspersed with foul language.

When she ran out of breath, Walker said, "Give me your car keys. I'm taking some evidence away and posting officers at every door of this house. I'd advise you not to attempt to leave until I return for you. You may call an attorney and pack what you need for staying in jail until, and unless, you can make bail."

He didn't mention that the "officers" consisted only of Ron Parker.

It was five days later before everyone could get together to hear all the details of the two murder cases that turned out to be connected. It had taken that long for Howard and Chief Simpson to receive all the forensic reports.

By coincidence, it was the same day that Lily and Robert were hosting a rather silly celebration dinner at Grace and Favor. Earlier that day, the prohibition of wine and beer had been repealed. Not that many at the dinner, or in Voorburg, or the rest of the country, had observed that pesky law since Roosevelt had been elected. Everyone had felt sure that the new President would repeal the law.

All the residents of Grace and Favor, as well as Howard, Miss Twibell, Jack Summer and his cousin Ralph, were there. Howard refused to explain anything until they'd finished dinner and dessert and moved on to a big dusty bottle of fine old champagne that Robert had located in the basement.

"A toast to the best Chief of Police in New York, if not the whole country," Robert said when their glasses were all filled.

Howard thanked them, and made his own toast. "To Miss Lily Brewster, who suggested the key to all the crimes."

"It wasn't deliberate," Lily said, blushing furiously. "It was merely something trivial I'd noticed."

"What was that?" Mrs. Tarkington, dressed in her best dress and jewelry for the occasion, asked.

"That Mrs. Connor seemed to hate all men," Howard said. "It was the crucial key, even if I didn't recognize it when she said it. And what's more, Lily was the one who bearded the dragon in her den, bought the typewriter, and spotted the final piece of evidence—the long black coat and the black fur hat the hiker had seen a man wearing.

"It wasn't a man, of course," Howard said. "It was a tall, strong woman. The hiker admitted he hadn't seen the person's face. But we all assumed it was a man, until Lily saw the hat and coat in one the boxes of things Mrs. Connor meant to take with her when she moved out. Then everything started to fall into place."

He continued, "Deputy Parker from Beacon found the shotgun hidden under some hay in the barn. Mrs. Connor's coat, the treads on the bottom of her boots, and the trunk of her automobile where she'd put the shotgun to take home and hide, were analyzed, and contained exactly the same nasty ooze that surrounds the foul lake. It's a good thing she apparently hadn't worn the boots again last winter. It would have seriously muddled the evidence."

"You couldn't have found this out a hundred years ago," Jack Summer commented. "Probably back then nobody even knew about the science of fingerprinting."

Phoebe had a question. "What was the typewriter thing about?"

Howard explained that a nurse had supposedly typed a letter about the older boy, Aidan, who had reportedly gone to New York City. "She typed a letter to Aidan's parents saying he'd broken his right wrist, and assured them he'd write back as soon as it healed.

"The police chief of Beacon," Howard explained, "found out that no such hospital had ever existed. But Mrs. Connor's fingerprints were all over the typewriter Lily bought. And also all over the envelope, and the letter from the made-up hospital and mythical nurse. The only other fingerprints on it were Aidan's father's, who'd opened the envelope and read the letter to his wife. What's more, the letter had a slight crooked letter 'a' and so did the typewriter."

Mrs. Prinney said, "I could imagine murdering a husband if I had one like Mrs. Connor had—if I were as nasty as she was. But I simply can't believe she'd kill one grandson, and try to kill the only other one she had. Though it sounds as if the evidence proves it."

"I don't think the charge of trying to blow up Kelly's bus will hold, though," Howard said. "I know it was her, but there's no physical evidence that would hold up in court. With that mob of relatives of hers scattered all over the valley, someone probably told her where he was. I'm glad I was saved from having to hunt them all down to question them.

"I doubt that the charge against her for smothering her husband will hold up either. There's no physical proof. Though I'm convinced that was her, too."

Nobody else had anything to say that could explain how Mrs. Connor could have had such hatred for her only grandchildren. But after a short silence, Robert asked, "How is Kelly taking the fact that he's inherited a farm?"

"He doesn't want it," Howard said. "He says he enjoys the job he has. He likes meeting lots of new people and traveling around. He doesn't want the hard work, the huge investment in machines and tools, and the headache of trying to find a good workforce. He's going to sign over a quitclaim to his father and mother when he turns eighteen next month. He thinks they'll sell it, sight unseen, and move to a better climate."

Howard went on, "I know I can trust all of you not to gossip about this. And Jack, I'm sure, will stick to the bare facts without personal embellishments, won't you?"

Jack nodded. "I'm not a yellow journalist. You know I'll stick to the facts."

"One more toast," Miss Twibell said. "To Kelly Connor."